Broken Lies
Sarah Lewin
© 2025

This book is dedicated to:

My four beautiful grown-up children
– you are my world, even though you live far away.
I'll never be able to show or tell you how much I love you.
I love each of you to the moon, the stars and back
and I am so proud of the amazing adults you are.

Chapter One

I ran until my feet ached, thick socks and big black shoes rubbing uncomfortably with every step. The footwear I wore for work at the library wasn't suited to running. I panted, drops of sweat dripped off my brow and ran down my cheeks. Their salty taste made me gag as they reached my tongue. The concrete footpath reflected the heat of the sun, even in autumn. Passersby on the street paid me no attention. Most were at least twenty years older than my thirty years, preoccupied with their own problems. As I reached the train station, I watched in horror as the train I needed pulled away.

"Damn!"

I found a quiet spot near the ticket counter and leant against the dirty brick wall to catch my breath. In the distance I heard a busker. The soulful violin tune caused my stomach to tighten. Only one train a day passed through West Haven, heading to the big city and the airport. My opportunity to connect with the one person who might lead me to my child had just disappeared in the plume of smoke kicked up by the train wheels.

I jumped as a hand touched my arm. "Are you okay Scarlett?" My old English teacher, Mrs Paisley, her grey hair pinned bun high in a bun, stood just to my right, trundling a small suitcase.

"Yes, thank you. I came here to say goodbye to someone, but I missed the train." I tried to be as truthful as possible. I'd graduated more than ten years ago, but it didn't feel right, lying to a teacher.

"I've ordered a taxi if you want to ride back with me," my old teacher said brightly. "I've just come back from a few days at the beach with my daughter. We always have such a delightful time."

"Amy is lovely." We'd been friends during primary school and the start of high school, until we'd pursued different hobbies and taken different subjects. Amy chose basketball, history, and archaeology. I picked swimming, English, and drama. "Thanks for the offer, but I'm going to walk back." It wasn't that far.

My teacher smiled. "I'll tell Amy I ran into you. Next time she visits, maybe you two can catch up. Did you know she works at a museum in the city?"

"I kept up with her activities through social media. It would be nice to meet up with her in person," I acknowledged.

After seeing Mrs Paisley safely into the taxi, I headed back to work. My black shoes kicked the dry dirt and small rocks as I took the long way back to town. Anxiety, or fear, made it difficult to decide if my decisions were valid, or if I was constantly over-reacting.

My mind ran through the events of the last few days.

I could have approached things differently. By pure chance, I overheard a conversation in the library a couple of days ago.

"I returned to town for my sister's funeral," said an older gentleman, dressed in a bowler hat, three-piece grey suit, and maroon tie, leaning wearily on his walking stick. I imagined him to be an English Professor, or maybe a distinguished mystery novelist.

"Are you Margo Watson's brother?" young Noah, our work experience teen, asked as he mis-shelved yet another book. From my position, returning the children's games parents had borrowed before story time, I could see that a book on origami didn't belong in the cooking section. I tutted, resisting the urge to fix the error in front of a customer.

The whole town knew Margo Watson, she was integral in establishing the local art society, the local women's craft group, and the little athletics club.

"She taught my mother how to crochet, I think," Noah added.

"My sister helped a lot of people," the grandly dressed gentleman agreed. "Still, I didn't expect so many to attend her funeral. They filled the church, with others standing outside during the service." He held his hand out and shook the teen's hand. "My name is Gerald Watson. I'm only in town for a few days; I'm due to return home by the end of the week. While I'm here, can you point me in the direction of some local history books? My stepson Brandon jokes that West Haven is boring, and I want to prove him wrong. Brandon Kelly – you'd be too young to know him; he only lived here for a short period."

This gentleman was Brandon Kelly's stepfather! How could this nice looking, kind, elderly man be related to such an obnoxious, rude, bully?

A few minutes later, once my heart had slowed a little, I made my way over to the local history section with a pile of magazines to place in the nearby stand.

"Good afternoon, can I help you with anything?" I asked the older man. Standing closer to him I thought he may give off the same sinister vibes as his stepson. Instead, his aura emitted a mix of calmness and strength. I didn't detect any unpleasant aspects to his character. But then, his stepson fooled me. I only bore the brunt of his true personality after it was too late.

Gerald Watson turned towards me, his right hand moving slightly on his cane, steadying himself. "Hello there. I used to live here. I grew up in West Haven, a long time ago." He smiled a little, the lines on his face giving away his age. "I'm keen to read about some of the local history, to refresh my memory of this quaint village. My sister refused to leave West Haven, she spoke so highly of the people who live here. I thought it might be interesting to tell my son and grandson about the town where I grew up."

My stomach tightened. I clenched my toes deep in my shoes, gripping the magazines so tightly my fingernails dug into the glossy covers. He lived with Brandon and his son, my son! My instinct stopped me from revealing my identity. "My favourite book about West Haven is this one." I pulled a hardcover coffee table book with full colour photographs. "It includes stories of some of our famous ancestors, a movie star, a poet, and a couple of athletes. Oh, and you may remember the annual harvest festivals, there are some terrific anecdotes."

I left Gerald to peruse the local history books and returned to my work shelving returns. The routine went some way to calming me. I concentrated on breathing in through my nose, out through my mouth. My job, the library, the one place where I was safe, where I didn't let worry and anxiety takeover. I focused on that peace, the calm, the order, the routine.

An hour later, after my boss Eve, and I locked the library doors, she headed to the supermarket and I headed to my favourite café, The Black Pot. Visiting the café each afternoon had become a routine that helped to ease my anxiety. Owned and managed by my best friend of over twenty years. He'd make me a large mug of mocha, choose a sweet treat for me, and let me sit quietly, or talk about my day.

I stared into my mug, still half full of coffee and chocolate. Archie, my oldest friend, nd local barista, looked at me with sympathy. His sandy coloured hair cut short now, still reminded me of the long-haired teen who loved nothing better than to play music on his electric blue guitar. "I mean, I wanted to tell him I'm Leo's mother, but I'm clearly not a great judge of character, present company excepted," I added quickly as Archie pretended to throw a tea towel at me. "I didn't pick Brandon was a psychopath. Just because I think this kindly little old man, is, well, a kindly gentleman, it doesn't mean he's not hiding some evil side."

Archie rubbed the coffee machine with the tea towel, until the metal gleamed. "Yes, but he is Margo Watson's brother. That's like celebrity status around here. The Watsons are all philanthropists. You did say Brandon is his stepson, which means they're not blood related." My best bud had a way of calming me down. His sensible approach to life meant he'd owned The Black Pot for years, while I'd managed to half finish three degrees, and only landed the job of assistant librarian because no one else more suitable applied. I felt his deep blue eyes on me, assessing my mental state.

"True," I mused, drinking the rest of the delicious mocha. Archie always made it just right. He had a knack for brewing perfect drinks, which is why customers flocked to the café, even now, late in the afternoon, on their way home from work.

Archie handed a takeaway cup to Oliver, one of our old school mates who now taught at the primary school we'd once attended. I nodded at him as he left in a hurry, his two young ones fighting over a bag of donuts. "Do you even know it's the same Brandon Kelly?" Archie asked quietly. On my left, blonde Carrie, one of the local gossips, leant over the counter, advising Pippa, who worked at the cafe after school, on how to choose the perfect macaroon.

I eyed him sceptically. "There's more than one?" I'd met Brandon at university, during my first attempt at a degree. I thought I wanted to be a doctor, but I knew within a semester it wasn't for me. "I suppose it's possible, though I'm not convinced. Maybe I should do some investigating, to make sure it's the same Brandon. Gerald Watson referred to Brandon as having lived in West Haven for a time. Brandon never told me that he lived here." Why wouldn't he tell me that, when we were dating? I told him everything about me.

Archie looked at me, the concern and care obvious, even before he spoke. "Are you sure you want to go sleuthing? You've been in a good place recently. Why don't we go out for a nice dinner instead? We could make it a date." He grinned.

My best friend, or annoying side kick, with his wavy blondish hair, deep blue eyes and slightly freckled skin, had always been popular. The girls at school used to call him spunky, and he still possessed that boyish charm that drew customers into his café. I, on the other hand, had a shock of deep red hair, as my name suggested, and green eyes. My mother was a fan of epic love stories, while I preferred dark mysteries and gothic dramas.

"We've been out of school ten years this year. We've eaten dinner together hundreds of times, you might want to rethink your words," I said with a grin. It was our standing joke that one day I'd relent and let him take me on a real date. It was never going to happen. I valued our friendship far too much.

The café door swung open, and a group of older women bustled in, each wore an orange silk scarf. "I'll leave you to it. Watch out for the book club ladies. They'll drink all your coffee and eat all your macaroons." I grinned at Archie, as I held the door open for the women. They knew Archie and I by name, and while he would be greeting them individually, I knew them simply as the book club, though I did try to remember the books they liked. I made a note to make more of an effort to pay attention.

Home was only a five-minute walk away. Not the big old house I grew up in. After finishing high school, I left town to attend university in the city. I ditched medicine quickly; and lost interest in my second choice just as fast. Turned out an arts degree wasn't challenging enough. My third, and final attempt was an online creative writing course.

When I returned to West Haven, I found a cute one-bedroom cottage to rent. The weatherboard exterior could use a fresh coat of paint. So could the internal walls, but all things considered I was lucky.

Long term rentals were rare in town, especially this close to work, and at a reasonable price.

The landlord didn't allow pets, something about hair all over the house, so I settled for putting seeds out for the local birds. One willy wagtail in particular liked to perch on the verandah railing, greeting me as I returned home each afternoon.

"What a day Willy," I told him, as I slipped out of my black shoes, without untying the laces. "What do you think? Should I track down Mr Watson, pour my heart out and tell him his stepson is a mean bully who stole my baby?"

Willy tilted his head, just a little, as if considering my question. He pecked at the nearly empty saucer, collecting the last few seeds left behind by a day's worth of visiting sparrows and pigeon doves. Some days I thought it'd all been a bad dream. Leo was only a few days old when Brandon stole him from the hospital while I slept. His caesarean birth took more out of me than I could've imagined. When I realised Leo had been taken, I became hysterical and ended up temporarily in the mental ward at the hospital. My parents and doctors agreed it would be better if I stayed medicated, rather than searching for my son. Even under sedation the ache in my heart rivalled the pain in my milk filled bosom and post-partum body.

"I know it happened. My boy would be nearly four now," I whispered, the intensity of my emotions threatening to return. Willy looked around, before flying up into the nearest tree, a large eucalypt.

I waited for the tell-tale salty tears to reach my lips. Whenever I let my mind wander to wonder how Leo would look now, whether he had my colouring, green eyes, what his first words were, when he walked, water stung my eyes. This time, when I raised my fingers to my cheeks, they remained dry. I'd cried so many tears for the first two years; I probably used my lifetime quota. My stomach would cramp, my hands would shake, I'd survived on coffee and chocolate for such a long time.

Disappeared without a trace. The kindly policeman told me after he spoke with the nurses, watched the hospital security footage and performed whatever passed as nominal police investigations.

Probably for the best. Agreed a well-meaning doctor who diagnosed me with post-natal depression. She didn't quite say that Leo would be better off with his father, but it had been clearly implied. After I was released from the mental ward, I refused the sleeping pills, and the calming tablets. I declined to talk to any more professionals. Therapy wasn't going to help me find my son.

I'd met Brandon at university. Dark hair, broody brown eyes, studying law, I fell hard for the mysterious stranger. He lived off campus in a rental property. That he was interested in a small-town girl like me spun my head. It didn't help that I didn't find university interesting, I happily played into his plan.

After an incident in high school, I was innocent, gullible, and ready to believe he loved me. My parents all but disowned me, after I'd fallen in with the wrong crowd, developed a liking for alcohol, and spiralled into a depression. High functioning anxiety and alcohol was a bad mix.

I thought back to the days after I came out of hospital. As was the case after my drunken debacle, Archie was the only person who stood by me. By the time the doctors released me from hospital, more than a week had passed since Brandon stole Leo from the crib in plain view of the nurses. I went looking for him and my baby but found no trace of either of them. Left with limited options I returned to the town I knew.

Had I known Brandon had lived here, however briefly, I may have changed how I approached the search. Then again, I'd expected sympathy from my parents. I walked over to the photo of my newborn baby, the only photograph I had of my child. *What would I have done differently? What could I have done differently? If I'd not let fear take control. If my parents had been supportive. Hindsight won't help us, neither will regret. I will find you one day Leo. I've missed so much of your life already...*

I walked away from the photo, not because I wanted to break the only connection with Leo, but talking wouldn't solve my dilemma. My parents, both self-absorbed, busy with their own lives, and expected me to do the same. Their one piece of advice was to get on with my life and to stop being dramatic. They never got over the embarrassment of my anxiety, and my one alcoholic mishap. Quick to judge and slow to forgive, when I told them about Brandon taking Leo, they accused me of *telling stories in order to attract attention.* They expressed a huge disappointment in my inability to finish a degree and couldn't understand why I didn't just get a job and get on with life. Neither would openly consider the option that I had given birth to a son I'd lost to a narcissist. Their more reasonable explanation was I'd lost the baby, if I'd even been pregnant.

Every day, for more than two years, Archie would visit and make sure I had food, and coffee. That I ate real food, not just chocolate. He let me talk about Leo, without judgement. He indulged my depression, anxiety and fears, to a point. Most of my waking hours I spent trolling the internet for images of Brandon and Leo. I looked for any social media presence or evidence of their existence. I hardly slept, and when I did the nightmares drove me to the edge. Archie encouraged me to read, rather than googling, or watching sad movies. He gently suggested a daily walk, or some form of physical activity.

After the first twelve months I decided that looking for Leo was driving me mad, and if I didn't stop internet searching, for Leo and Brandon, I'd end up in the loony bin, or gaol. I stopped internet stalking any lead I could find and instead started reading books on dealing with trauma and how to heal. I ventured out, as far as Archie's café, once a day for a cuppa and a sweet treat. I also stopped trying to talk to my parents.

Eventually I stopped talking about my baby, even to Archie. I still spoke to Leo, every day when I woke up, and every night as I fell asleep.

It kept me sane. That, Archie's café, and my job at the library. Did I want to jeopardise it all?

In a heartbeat, Leo, if I thought I'd get to see you, to love you, to look after you. Is your grandfather a nice man? Would he carry a message to you, or better still, would he tell me where you live?

Checking the water level in the kettle, I made a coffee, sat at my kitchen table and stared at my laptop screen. My fingers punched the name Brandon Kelly into the search bar. "I know," I said aloud to myself, "I promised myself I wouldn't, and I haven't, but I want to know...if there's even a chance...I have to know."

As I stretched my legs a couple of hours later, I heard footsteps on the verandah. "Only me!" I recognised Archie's voice instantly. "I figured you'd forget to eat, so I grabbed some burgers and chips." He placed two cardboard boxes on the table. "No need for plates," he added as I fussed around the kitchen. "Sit down, grab a sugar and salt laden fast-food item and tell me what you discovered."

The cardboard box from the local fish and chip shop revealed a surprisingly tasty looking burger and crispy potato chips. "Thanks for this, and how did you know I'd be researching anything?" I tried to look serious, but my friend was grinning. He was just as cute now as when we were at school. I couldn't deny that. He stared at me over his burger. I returned the look, munching on mine. Turned out I was starving. I savoured the taste of lettuce, cheese, tomato, egg, and beetroot, alongside the beef patty. Once I'd eaten pretty much all the burger and over half my chips, I answered Archie's question. "Yes, okay, you're right. It's the same Brandon Kelly. I'd not searched for Leo, for so long, because, well, you know...Anyway, so there's that." I heard the tremor in my voice. "Coffee?" I said with as much brightness as I could muster.

"Go on then, and if you still have some chocolate biscuits a couple of those would be nice. I didn't eat any of the profits today. I'm sticking to my new year's resolution." Archie collected the food wrappers, tipping them into the plastic grey bin by my back door as I made our cuppas. He certainly didn't need to limit his food intake. His speedy metabolism and long hours at work meant he'd not an ounce of fat on his body.

"New year's resolution?" I scoffed. "We're nearly halfway through the year already." I rarely saw him eat any of the goodies he sold, unless he was sitting, trying to convince me to eat.

A beep on my phone told me I had mail. I didn't bother reading it, I'd check it later. I often received email offers from authors, to read and review their latest books. During my hermit days I'd built up quite a lot of social media author friends. I occasionally read, reviewed or helped in marketing their books.

"Do you want to play a card game, or one of the board games?" Archie indicated the coffee table with the long drawers. He'd been my saviour during my darkest days, sitting up with me for hours playing scrabble, uno, monopoly, rummy, and when we got sick of those, he helped me with jigsaws.

I placed the deep blue mugs on the table, and a plate of mint chocolate biscuits. "Best of three?" I suggested grabbing a deck of cards.

Five hands later I admitted defeat with a yawn. "I'll win next time," I threatened good naturedly, knowing it wasn't likely. I waved goodbye at the door, as Archie walked half a block away, to the house he inherited from his nan.

As I turned out the light, my mobile beeped again, reminding me of my unread email. I opened my inbox on my laptop, dropping onto a chair as I read the words on the screen.

Don't try to find us. If you persist – you'll regret it.

Chapter Two

The more I ran, the more they chased me. The same nightmare, every night. The ghostly figures with angry, ghoulish faces ran faster than I. As their cold, long fingers reached and touched my skin, I'd wake in a cold sweat. Sometimes I was running in the forest, or along a city street. Occasionally I'd find myself crawling through tunnels in old houses, or weird shops with circus carnival faces.

My heart thumped so loudly I thought I was having a heart attack. I hit the snooze button on my alarm clock. With my head down between my knees I took some deep breaths, counting down from one hundred. I refused to see a doctor for my anxiety. Pills were out of the question too. I preferred to use the techniques I found in books. I'd learnt a lot, about how to calm my emotions and fears. By the time my alarm beeped again I felt calmer. Then I remembered the email.

Don't try to find us. If you persist – you'll regret it.

I had no idea how Brandon would've known I'd been considering looking for him. As I waited for the kettle to boil, I eyed my laptop. It's not likely Brandon could've bugged it; I'd bought it after I'd returned home from the city. Maybe his stepfather mentioned he'd be attending his sister's funeral in West Haven. I briefly wondered if you could set an alert that warned if someone googled your name?

Did I want to find Brandon? Only because he would lead me to Leo. Was I strong enough to stand up to Brandon, and fight for my son? My parents would be no support. Archie would help in any way he could, but I didn't want to jeopardise his business, his livelihood...I sighed. This was something I had to do myself. Or not. I had a day to decide if I'd seek out Gerald Watson before he returned home.

The thing I loved most about my job, was the number of books I had access to. The interactions with others who loved make believe worlds as much as I did was a bonus. The morning flew by with little opportunity to worry about Brandon's threat. Story time with the little ones and their parents, followed by IT lessons for the oldies, and time to shelve books before my lunch break.

Normally I'd have brought a salad wrap and fruit from home. Routine, habit, calm, peaceful, the same ritual every day, kept me sane. Today wasn't normal, I'd forgotten to pack my lunch. I contemplated visiting the café. Archie would worry, and I didn't need that on my conscience. Telling him about the threatening email wasn't an option. Not yet anyway.

Choosing café food over supermarket food wasn't the healthiest of meal choices, not that I'd dream of telling Archie. Less than a block from the library, the short walk in the sunshine to the supermarket helped. The vitamin D, warm on my skin, the sound of the magpies warbling, even the few cars, and the window shoppers helped me smile through my anxiety.

Only a few people took advantage of their lunch time to buy groceries. Grateful for that, I wandered the aisles, trying to decide that to buy. I chose grapes, and picked a bag of nuts, and some berries. As I passed the freezer section I noticed Gerald Watson chatting to Jenny Wilson. Jenny's family were locals, and she was a friend of my mother. The lump in my throat, made swallowing difficult. Should I interrupt them and introduce myself to Gerald? Or wait and find an opportunity to talk to him when their conversation ended? I could loiter around the checkout after my purchase; in the hope Gerald wouldn't be long.

Instead, I hurried past them to the check out, opting for the serve yourself machine. I added a bottle of water to my purchases. My heart pounded as I pictured talking to Gerald in front of my mother's friend. A backward glance told me they were still deep in conversation, so I headed back to work.

Living in the same town for most of my life was both comforting and annoying. Small enough that gossips knew everyone and made up stories to start rumours. I didn't want my parents to hear I'd been badgering Gerald Watson to find my son. On the positive side, I knew where most places were, and could find my way around. I vaguely knew a lot of people, though not by name. Many of my peers enjoyed close friendships, and many had left, to pursue careers in the bigger cities.

Being that nervous, nerdy child, before anxiety and emotions was the norm, didn't make me a popular choice for long lasting friendships. That suited me fine. My plan to leave West Haven and never return would have succeeded. Except for my inability to complete a degree, falling for the wrong guy, becoming pregnant, and having my child stolen. Choosing to return home for family support, wasn't the best decision of my life. Some days I still fantasized about leaving for good and disappearing into the anonymity of a big city.

Archie and Eve, my job, and my cute cottage, were reasons to stay. Bringing Leo up in West Haven would be nice. He could go to the same school I did, spend time with his grandparents, Archie, and Eve. We'd make an eclectic family.

"It's difficult to tell if my parents are upset, angry with me, or just don't care," I'd told Archie. His café became a pseudo-office for me, back then, when I gave in to his suggestion of finding employment and I trolled the job wanted sites. "Dad's always away in some third world country helping to build schools or hospitals. Mum's tour schedule is just as busy."

"Your parents worked hard in their chosen field," he agreed cautiously. "I remember your dad as the kindest, gentlest of doctors, when I broke my arm falling off the monkey bars. Your mum's artwork is off the charts unique." He looked uncomfortable, I knew he wanted to say something, but worried about my mental health.

"Just say it, I'm not going to meltdown. It's been weeks since I've had an episode." My voice wavered, so I frowned, to accentuate the fact that I was fine.

"Maybe, they don't know how to help you? What if they're broken hearted that their only grandchild was stolen before they even met him." Archie was saved from any more speculation as new customers chose that moment to enter for their morning tea.

I wanted to agree with Archie, to believe that my parents were devastated and that explained the emotional chasm between us. But I knew them well enough to know that if they felt that way, they'd leave no stone unturned, until they found their grandson.

Since my return nearly four years ago. I only spoke to my parents on special occasions; birthdays, Christmas, Easter, and if we ran into each other in town. Sticking to my routine was safe. I wasn't healed from the trauma of losing Leo, but I could survive if I stayed in my lane. Home, work, coffee shop. A walk in the park on weekends. Not looking on the internet to try to locate Brandon and Leo. I filled my time reading mystery novels, and I almost always guessed the ending.

"ARE THE GRAPES ANY good?" Eve interrupted my thoughts, as I sat in the library kitchenette pondering my next steps. My boss stood taller than me, a thin as a sapling tree, with short greying hair she bleached blonde. My guess was that she was probably a few years older than me. Wearing a black pants suit with a bright pink jacket, she exuded a sense of style I admired. Matching pink shoes, flats, she didn't need to wear heels, she towered above most of our patrons.

"They are delicious." I held up the container. "Help yourself, I'll never eat them all."

"Thanks," Eve's long slender fingers choose a bunch of green grapes. "Are you okay Scarlett? You're a little quiet today."

I faked a yawn. "I stayed up late reading," I fibbed. Eve had interviewed me, over a year ago, and despite my dishevelled look as the effects of no sleep, no money, and high anxiety, had taken a chance on me. I wondered if she too had survived some catastrophic trauma in her past. She wasn't local, not in the sense of having lived here most of her life. I didn't want to pry, but I was curious. Maybe one day I'd ask her. Over a coffee and a cake.

"Why didn't you say so? I'll make you some coffee and bring it out to you at the desk. I've got meetings with council most of the afternoon." She patted my shoulder, before turning away and checking the water level in the kettle.

"Thanks Eve. I can lock up tonight if you like. That way you can go straight home from your meetings." It wasn't like I had anywhere else to be. Archie's café would still be open after the library closed for the evening. Plus, I wanted Eve to know she could trust me, count on me to take added responsibility when she needed me to.

"I knew I made the right decision, employing you," Eve beamed. She picked out five more grapes, placing them on the plate that held her cheese and apple. She poured hot water into both mugs.

"I thought I was the only candidate." I grinned back.

THE AFTERNOON FLEW by as quickly as the morning, with a steady stream of people returning and borrowing books. Having lived in West Haven for most of my life, meant I knew many of the library customers. The library was busy enough to keep me from being preoccupied by my problems, but not busy enough to be run off my feet.

When I first returned, I'd imagined that everyone was whispering and talking about me, pointing their fingers and laughing about my misfortune. *That's Scarlett Nightly, lost her baby to a bully, or worse, she imagined the whole thing...Her parents are so ashamed, pity she couldn't make a go of university. Studying for a degree would have kept her out of trouble...no wonder her parents want nothing to do with her...*

"Have you ever thought about writing daytime soap operas?" Archie would say when I told him what I imagined people saying behind my back. "You know most people don't care about what's happening with other people, they're too busy trying to cope with their own dramas," Archie told me each time I freaked out that someone was staring at me.

My friend was right, I realised, eventually. Strangely, I found it easy to strike up conversations in the library. Here I wasn't Scarlett Nightly, but the assistant librarian. Apart from occasional comments like "Aren't you Tom and Dora's daughter?" most of the conversations focused on books, authors, and new releases.

We hosted story time for preschoolers, study help for teens, IT support for oldies, book club, writers' group, chess competitions, and school holiday activities. Eve and I had discussed additional experiences for patrons. We made a great team, full of energy, enthusiasm, and ideas.

Our library building had received a makeover a few years before I started working there. Still the same outer brick façade. The renovations inside were impressive. Gone were the individual room like spaces. Instead, an open area divided into creative, warm, welcoming areas. I appreciated the lighter, brighter, airy feel. As a child I loved pretending I was hiding from monsters in between the dark wooden shelves. Cushions and comfy chairs replaced the older, less comfortable seats. As an adult I preferred to be able to easily see and check for readers tucked away in the quiet corners. Especially when I was on close duty.

I saw the problem in the back corner of the reading space, only after I'd made sure everyone was out, and I'd locked the front door. The cart that held the books to be shelved first thing the next morning was covered in red paint.

Chapter Three

"You're late!" Archie handed me a large takeaway cup and a plate with a large piece of chocolate brownie. "Hang on, are you okay?" He touched my arm lightly, noticing the sweat still on my brow.

"Thanks for this, I might just sit down, if you don't mind." My legs felt a little wobbly and I wasn't sure my knees wouldn't buckle. I didn't want to drop the mocha and chocolate cake.

Archie's eyes searched mine. I recognised the worry in his. I'd caused him too much concern already. I didn't mean to be high maintenance. Before he could ask, the bell above the door jangled signifying more customers. I slid into the nearest booth, while my friend went into full on barista mode. His boyish good looks, charm, and skills with the coffee machine largely contributed to the success of The Black Pot.

A few deep breaths later, and I sensed my body was getting back to some semblance of normality. I nibbled on the brownie. Amazing, as always. Archie inherited his cooking skills from his mum, and his nan. I sipped the mocha. Coffee and chocolate both relaxed and energised me. I kept my breathing exercise up, hoping my logic brain came up with a reasonable explanation for the events of the last half hour.

"Okay, spill." Archie slid into the seat opposite me. He placed a bottle of water and a strawberry donut on the table in front of me. "I can tell something happened. Don't keep it all bottled up."

I drew in a breath, letting it escape as a sigh. "It sounds silly, saying it out loud. Someone spilt red paint on a trolley of books. A warning, I think. On top of an email last night to stop looking for them." I heard my voice tremble. I bit my lip.

Archie touched my arm. My skin tingled under his touch. Platonic friends, always, except for one night back in high school. We'd agreed then to stay friends, lest we ruin our friendship by getting more involved. I could sense he was upset for me, worried about me, but he always kept calm. He knew it was the best way to quieten my anxiety. "You've got a form of PTSD, because of what happened to you. You have anxiety, but you're not crazy, nor does anything you said sound silly. Did the email have a sender?" Archie broke the donut in half, taking a bite of the half he kept in his hand. "I hope you took photographs of the mess in the library."

"I'll admit, I didn't study the email, or look at it, since opening it last night. I wasn't sure what to do and decided to ignore it." I shook my head slowly from side to side. "I think I've decided to find Gerald and talk to him. I'll tell him who I am and ask if he'll tell me where Brandon and Leo are. Even after receiving the email. But, then the paint..."

"Photos?" Archie encouraged slowly. The bell jangled, as the last of the customers in the café left.

My hands shook as I took my mobile from the pocket of my cardigan and handed it to Archie. "I think I got a couple of decent photos." I drank the rest of my mocha. "I'm feeling a little better now. I need to go back and clean it up."

"Wait for me, and I'll help," he suggested as he scrolled through my photos. "It looks like the paint spells the word '*Stop*.'

I could have kissed my friend. "You think so? I thought I saw the word too but told myself I was being ridiculous. Can I borrow a bucket and some paper towel? I'm good to clean it myself, I'll bring these back when I finish." I hoped I sounded braver than I felt.

Archie looked at me. "If you're sure, I'm still open for half an hour. When you come back, we'll work out something for dinner." He stood, as the bell jangled above the door.

ARMED WITH A BUCKET, and a roll of paper towel I headed back to the library. I let myself in through the back door, turning on all the lights as I did so. My heart thumped in my chest. "I can do this," I whispered aloud. "There's nothing to be scared of," I let my voice grow louder, as I moved through the empty building. "I am safe, I am strong, I am sane."

The book trolley contained approximately twenty books for shelving. Most of the paint was contained to the top shelf. The books on the bottom had a couple of small drops of red. Luckily, with a little elbow grease, I managed to easily clean those spots off without any further damage. The ten books on the top shelf were more badly damaged. The paint did indeed appear to spell the word *Stop*. I took a few more photos, my hands steadier than before. I laid the books out onto the nearest table and added a tiny amount of dishwashing liquid to the water in the bucket. Ever so slowly, the red paint faded and eventually disappeared from the spines of the books. "Right, you lot can dry there overnight. I'll be in early tomorrow morning to check on you." Talking out loud when I was alone helped me feel more in control.

In a text to Eve, I let her know there'd been an accident with some paint, but that it was all under control. I re-locked the door, ensuring the alarm was set. Clutching the now empty bucket in my right hand, I counted each step towards the café. Focusing on the numbers stopped me from freaking out. I mean, how could Brandon know I'd considered searching for him and Leo, and as he wasn't in town, how he did manage to coerce someone else to mess with the library books?

"Don't tell me you're counting again," Archie said kindly, as he stepped in front of me. "How do tacos sound? For dinner I mean. We'll make it taco Tuesday. I'll pick up ingredients on the way to your place."

I rubbed my forehead with the palm of my hand. "Yes, counting, old habits, sorry." I tried to bend my lips into a smile. "Tacos sound perfect. Can I grab the ingredients, while you close the café?" I handed Archie the bucket and the remaining paper towel and left, before he had a chance to ask me any more questions.

Returning to the supermarket for the second time in the day, I focused on the task at hand. The shop was crowded, people shopping for food on their way home from work. Children in uniform, pyjamas, or sports gear, were competing for their parents' attention, waving sugar laden food in front of them. I slipped past groups of friends chatting, families debating dinner options, and staff stacking items on shelves. I knew what aisles I needed. Part of my healing had been to map out the items I commonly used, to make trips to the supermarket less overwhelming. In my head I knew the list of ingredients for tacos, and quickly grabbed the taco shells, sauce, mince, avocados, salad, and cheese. I moved through the self-checkout without a problem.

I beat Archie to my place. The groceries put away, and the table set, I checked the mailbox, not expecting the letter that waited for me. Addressed to Scarlett Nightly, the return address surprised me. Sinclair Attorneys were the local firm of lawyers. I tore the letter open, expecting to read that I was being sued by Brandon, for...something....

Not quite sure I believed the words on the page, I re-read the letter, embossed with the Sinclair Attorneys official letterhead.

I am writing to formally invite you to the reading of the Last Will and Testament of the late Margo Watson. The will reading will be held on Wednesday 10 May at 10am. Please attend our office at 110 Wyn Way.

Chapter Four

I read the letter aloud to Archie, as he started preparing dinner. "You have to go," he told me in his serious, no-nonsense voice, as he fried the mince, garlic, and onion together in my frying pan.

I nodded. "Yeah, though I don't think I ever met Margo, and have no idea why I've been asked to attend the reading of her will. I think she and Mum were friends, or at least both travelled in the same social circles. I stopped paying attention to that sort of stuff a long time ago." I sipped a glass of water, willing the cooling liquid to calm me. "It still makes no sense, why I'd be included in her will." I drank some more water. "This must be linked – Gerald Watson, searching for Leo, the threatening email, paint on the books, and now the reading of the will. I know I can't afford to overthink it. I don't want to go back to how I was before." Barely being able to function, hiding under the covers, in my pyjamas all day. I refused to go back to that. Brandon wasn't going to rule my life.

"One step at a time," Archie agreed. "Dinner will be ready in five minutes. He turned towards me. "For what it's worth, I don't think you'll go back to the way you were before, you're stronger now. You have me, and Eve, and the job you love."

Archie was right. I could walk away from the Watsons, and be safe, and sane. I wanted Leo in my life as well. Was it selfish of me to think I could have it all?

HOURS LATER, AFTER winning at cards, shooing Archie home with promises that I was okay, I found myself sitting at my computer. This time I searched for Gerald Watson. He and his sister owned several properties across the state. Residential, and business holdings. Margo's four children lived across the country, with only one remaining locally. Gerald's family was a little more complicated. Three wives, five children, and three stepchildren, including Brandon Kelly. The minimal information available on the internet didn't provide a lot of answers. Despite my attempts, there was no definitive address for Brandon, or even Gerald. What I did find was details of some of the business interests they were involved in. I opened the bottom drawer of the dresser in the corner of the dining room. I extracted an old notebook and jotted down all the information I'd collected. Oddly satisfied at my research I made myself a hot chocolate. *"If there is a way that I can find you and bring you home, then I will,"* I told Leo's photograph.

I refused to give in to the melancholy. I'd missed so much of his life. *"I'll do what I can. If I can't find you now, I'll not give up. I promise,"* I whispered, kissing the photograph.

HOURS LATER I KICKED my blankets off. Sleep eluded me. Every time I closed my eyes I saw Brandon, with Leo. The more I ran after them, the further away they were, until finally they disappeared into a thick fog. I picked one of the books on my reading pile and curled up against my pillow. Soon I lost myself in the pages of a rom com.

I woke up five minutes before my alarm was due to beep. My anxiety levels were higher than they'd been for over a year, and I still hadn't decided if I was going to seek out Gerald before he returned to his home. I assumed he'd attend the will reading. An easier option may be to pull him aside afterwards and reveal myself as Leo's mother.

In the hour before I woke up properly, several versions of the scenario, where Gerald disappeared into a thick fog, vanished as soon as the door opened, or was whisked away by a black van played on repeat in my brain. "*This will work*," I told myself as I got myself ready for work. "*I can do this*," I repeated as I made my morning cuppa, breakfast and cobbled together the messiest peanut butter sandwich for lunch. My hands shook as I collected my keys, wallet, and phone, shoving them into my brown leather handbag, on top of my lunch box and drink bottle.

As I planned, I arrived at the library before Eve, so I could check on the books. "The paint has faded enough on all but two of them, that they should be okay to be shelved." I showed my boss when she arrived. "I'm sorry that I didn't see this happen, I'm not even sure where the red paint came from." I left out the part about the word *stop* emblazoned across the spines. "Also, weirdly, I have an invitation to go to Sinclair Attorneys at 10am this morning, for the reading of Margo Watson's will. I barely knew the woman, and I can't think why I must attend. If you don't mind, I'd like to go and see what it's about." Eve didn't know about Leo specifically, only that I'd experienced a deeply traumatic event. I forced my breathing to slow, hoping my heart would follow.

"Wednesday morning's normally quiet. I can hold the fort. I was going to see if you could close again this evening. I've another meeting this afternoon. The council want us to host a Book Week event, and I want to get a deeper understanding of their expectations. Then tomorrow, I'd like us to sit together and brainstorm it," Eve spoke slowly, which I knew meant she was excited at the prospect of the Book Week project, but didn't want to get her own hopes up. Or mine. She wore her red power suit, with the black singlet top, an indication she wanted to appear confident and positive during the meeting.

I glanced at my own attire. Somehow, I'd managed to remember her telling me about colours and how they affected our moods. I'd chosen a calming emerald-green shirt with my black pants. I'm not sure if the colour was calming me, although overall I felt a little more in control and confident than usual. "Book Week activities sound exciting. I'd love to get stuck into that project with you. Closing tonight won't be a problem. The will reading shouldn't take long."

The freak rainstorm overhead should have been an indication that the rest of the morning wasn't going to be easy. It happened often but I still got annoyed each time I was caught unawares. The huge droplets marked my dress shirt. Sinclair Attorneys was less than a block away, and the sun had returned from behind the cloud by the time I pushed open the door. Did I expect to see a handful of expectant people seated in the waiting area? Yes. Were there any? No.

The only other person in the room was the receptionist. "Scarlett Nightly?" She asked brightly, a customer service smile plastered firmly on her face.

"That's me," I told the middle-aged lady with short brown wavy hair. I glanced at my watch, worried I may have been late. I wasn't. Where was everyone else and how did this woman know who I was?

She stared at her computer screen, pushed a few keys on the keyboard in front of her. "Mr Sinclair will be with you shortly." She dismissed me with a wave of her hand, indicating the grey fake leather sofa behind me.

As I debated whether to sit, or continue to stand, the door to the left of the receptionist opened and a man, maybe ten years older than me, with snow white hair appeared. "Miss Nightly?" he asked in a tone indicating he knew the answer. "This way please." He motioned with his hand that I should enter the room behind him.

"I expected there to be more people here," I spoke as calmly as I could, above the thumping sound my heart was making.

"Please, take a seat," Mr Sinclair spoke firmly as he closed the door. My breakfast threatened to make a reappearance. I wasn't good with locked doors and closed rooms. "Margo Watson's will stipulated that each beneficiary be spoken to individually. As you'd expect, she had a long list of people in her life that she wanted remembered in some way."

I sat, deciding not to reveal that I hardly knew the woman. "I hoped to speak to Gerald this morning," I spoke in what I hoped was a conversational, and not confrontational manner. Some days I struggled with my tone. I felt like the kid that fell asleep in class and missed the lessons on how to communicate effectively with others.

"Ah, that's a shame. I think Mr Watson is planning to return home today. He was heading to the train station after he said his goodbyes to family and friends." Mr Sinclair's smile didn't move. I wondered if his face looked the same delivering good news or bad.

"Maybe you could remind me of his address, so I can write to him," I asked casually. My toes wiggled in the depths of my shoes, as the choice to speak to Leo's step grandfather seemed to be slipping away from me.

"I'm sure you'll understand and appreciate that I'm not able to give out that sort of information. If you contact the family, they'll be able to pass on your regards to him." The lawyer moved some papers around on his desk. "Margo's instructions to you were simple, I shouldn't need to keep you long." He read from the page in front of him. "To Scarlett Nightly, I leave this key to a safety deposit box located at the West Haven Bank. The entire contents of the safety deposit box are Scarlett's and hers alone. Please pass on to her my sincere apologies that I could not share the information with her in person." Mr Sinclair handed me a yellow envelope.

The envelope sat easily in my hand. My name printed neatly on the front. I turned the envelope over. The back contained no additional detail. I looked expectantly at the lawyer, waiting to see if there was anything else he was going to say.

He looked up from the papers on his desk. "Do you have any questions?"

"Did Margo have any other words, or instructions for me?" I wasn't sure what other questions to ask. I couldn't imagine what Margo kept for me in the safety deposit box.

Mr Sinclair stood. "I'm afraid that's all I have for you. Thank you again, for attending the office today."

I took my cue from his. "Thank you, for your time." I held out my hand to shake his.

As I left the office I debated my next move. Go back to work, as if nothing had changed. Go to the bank and access the safety deposit box. Or find Gerald Watson and ask him where my son was living. I consulted my mobile, looking for the train timetable. The only train to leave the station today was leaving the station in less than ten minutes.

Chapter Five

Just like that, my opportunity to find Leo, disappeared into thin air, as the train chugged along to its next destination. If I was lucky, the mystery box in the bank may provide some useful information. I checked my watch and sighed. That would have to be tomorrow's problem. I was due back at the library.

"I appreciate you stepping up, Scarlett," Eve said as I made us both coffees in the little kitchenette. "Did everything work out at Sinclair's? I'm not prying, I'm interested, but only if you're comfortable talking to me."

"Margo Watson left me something, some information, I think. It's in a safety deposit box. I'll go to the bank later this week. I'm not sure why, she left me anything. I knew her by reputation only." I paused, considering my words. I did trust my boss. "I know I haven't shared much with you, about what happened to me. I will one day. Why I fell apart, and how I'm still healing."

Eve squeezed my hand. "I understand. Just know that I'm here, if you ever want to talk."

THE LIBRARY WAS QUIET once the lunch crowd returned to their day jobs. Eve left for her meeting, and I found myself in front of the library's main computer. I considered searching for library members with the surname Kelly, or Watson, but that would breach a few personal and security laws.

Our library did contain an extensive microfiche collection. I wasn't sure what to search for, so I ran through old reels, looking for Watson or Kelly. A newspaper article from about six years ago caught my eye. A Watson family reunion. I recognised Brandon immediately. Other familiar faces in the photograph included my parents.

"I thought it odd at first," I told Archie over my late afternoon mocha, after locking the library with no further incident. "Then I remembered how much my parents like socialising, when they're not at work, or traveling."

Archie pushed the plate of macaroons closer to me. "Small towns. Everyone knows everyone. At least it feels like it."

"Does that mean someone in West Haven knows Brandon? Dumb question. Clearly, he is known in town, by the Watsons, and even my parents met him, at least once..."

"Sugar," Archie pushed the macaroons closer.

I smiled, a watery smile through stray tears, and reached for one of the delicious sugar treats. A pink one. "Yum," I nodded. "You should enter competitions with your baking. Seriously."

"Shucks Ma'am, you flatter me," he put on a funny accent, that had me giggling.

I picked up a light green macaroon, and crunched through the treat, following it with some more mocha. Eating more fruit, and green vegetables, when not at the café, might be a good idea. "I'm cautiously optimistic that I'll find some answers at the bank. I've made an appointment for tomorrow morning at 10am."

Archie returned to the counter and I people watched while finishing my treat. Were any of the patrons were related to Gerald, or Brandon? Pippa, with her long ginger braids, cleaned a spare table, chatting to the teens perched at the Wi-Fi counter. A well-dressed couple, both typing on laptops sat at a table in the middle of the café.

An older woman entered the café. I recognised her as Nettie Hill, a few years older than I, with a reputation of being a little loopy. Striding towards me, she screeched, "I know what you did!" as she pointed her finger at me. The other people in the café turned to look, but soon returned to their conversations, mobile phones, or laptops. The woman was well known around town for being crazy. Nettie's eyes stared with such anger, if I wasn't aware she was well known as being looney, I'd be freaking out right now.

The café door opened, signalling new customers. Archie moved out from behind the counter, gently steering Nettie towards the door as he did. "Brandon told me about you! Leave him alone!" she pointed her finger at me and continued to rant as he ushered her through to the footpath.

As my heart thumped like I'd been hit in the chest, I glanced around the café. No one seemed the least bit interested in Nettie's parting words. Archie raised his eyes, over the heads of his young customers. I gave him the thumbs up signal, trying desperately to get fresh air in my lungs.

When I met Brandon, he appeared confident, self-assured, and totally smitten with me. Open the door for me, watch rom coms with me, eat my favourite foods crazy about me. So sweet, considerate, and loving, that I thought nothing of moving in with him, within a few months. Once I did, things changed. My board and lodgings came with the expectation that I cook all his favourite foods, stay home and clean for him, and pretty much be at his beck and call.

He didn't physically hurt me. The verbal abuse was subtle. Telling me that couldn't cook properly, I was a stupid driver, that he was the only person who'd put up with me. He messed with my head, taking advantage of my anxiety.

Slowly the friends I made in the city got sick of me making excuses and stopped asking me to join them. By the time I realised I was pregnant, he pretty much had me all to himself. Never violent, the verbal abuse had been enough to keep me submissive, but I had no idea then just how badly his abuse affected me.

"Coercive control," Archie had said gently, when I'd eventually told him what happened. "The worst type of bully." Archie's choices when he left school was either study psychology or open a café. He studied psychology online while working in the café. As far as I could tell, both skills came in handy as owner of a successful coffee shop.

"It makes sense that Brandon convinced Nettie to ruin the books with paint," I whispered to Archie. I wasn't being paranoid. I knew only too well the power that man wielded.

Archie nodded, as he wiped down the tables around me. I'd offered to help, but he insisted I sit and eat more macaroons. Luckily for me I was blessed with a fast metabolism. I knew he was just trying to look after me. "Nettie was totally bonkers about some bloke who visited West Haven a while ago. She'd tell anyone who'd listen about her secret lover," he shuddered. "I thought it was all in her head."

"Maybe, or maybe that evil man decided to take advantage of her, to make sure I stay in my lane, and don't make a fuss." I polished off the last piece of deliciousness. "Which would have worked, except I seem to have found my fire, my determination."

"Your stubbornness," he quipped, ducking as I pretended to throw my napkin at him.

I stood. "Let me at least wash up for you and buy you dinner." I didn't wait for a response. I collected my plate and mug, and the couple of stray cups left on the Wi-Fi bench by the late afternoon coffee seekers. Archie, as much of a clean freak as I, had already washed most of the day's crockery and cutlery. Pippa tidied the eating area and wiped down most surfaces before she headed home. It took no more than a few minutes to complete the clean in the well-appointed kitchen.

A shiver ran down my spine as Archie moved into the space behind me, dropping his cleaning bucket and cloth into the second sink. It was a good tingle, not a scary shiver. It'd be easy to forget our vow to remain just friends. I pulled myself up to my full height, which still made me at least ten centimetres shorter than he. I looked into his eyes, trying to decipher the emotion I saw there.

"I'll cook chicken salad wraps," I tried for lightening the mood.

Archie laughed, "That's more like a jigsaw than actual, real cooking. Let me bring some ginger beer, and fruit kebabs...meet at yours in an hour."

"Done!" I let myself get carried away in the moment. "Shall I grab all the groceries, and we can assemble at mine?"

"I was going to suggest that. I need to run an errand first. I promised to deliver some cakes to Mr Brown. You remember out old science teacher? He broke his leg playing tennis and finds it difficult to get around. I offered to grab some groceries and drop them around after work." Archie shooed me out the door. "Get to the supermarket before it gets overrun with people hurrying home from work." He grinned mischievously. "I grabbed Mr Brown's groceries earlier in the day, when it was quiet."

Chapter Six

Too late. By the time I walked through the sliding doors, the supermarket was inundated with people. The queue for hot chickens, ready-made salads, bread products, and milk nearly made me turn around. "I'm not a quitter," I muttered quietly to myself. I didn't want to have to explain to Archie why there was no food. He'd understand, and he'd come and pick up what we needed, without complaining. I didn't want that. I wanted to be in control of my emotions enough to be able to grab groceries, hold down a full-time job, and look after my child.

I'd never be able to thank Archie enough, for everything he did while I got myself back from the edge. More patient than anyone else I'd ever met. He never asked for anything in return. I did sometimes worry that I was accidentally stopping him from moving ahead with his life, finding a girl and settling down. Something he'd wanted when we were teens. The same unconditional love his parents had. Devoted to each other and their child.

"There she is," I heard a snarly whisper and swung my head to see who they were talking about. Nettie stood with three other women I vaguely remembered from school. "She's the one. She bullied and scared Brandon away. He left town to raise his child, away from her crazy behaviour."

I turned away quickly, pretending to compare two types of salad. My cheek burned, as anger seethed just below the surface. How dare she spread lies about the situation. The truth was bad enough without getting caught up in make believe. Something in my brain snapped. They were talking about Leo, as Brandon's child, which was true, but he was just as much mine. I marched over to the group of women. "You don't know what you're talking about, Nettie. Brandon stole my child away from me." My hands shook, the anger in me seethed, so close to the surface I had to fight to be in control. "It's none of your business, any of you. If you're the one who vandalised the books in the library on Brandon's request, or if you do anything else, to me or anyone I know, I'll call the police."

The blood roared as it pumped around my body. I felt sure it'd explode, and Nettie would have the satisfaction of peeling me off the floor. I made myself calmly choose a packet of salad to go with the wraps and chicken already in my basket. I counted to twenty as I picked some fruit. It was only as I moved into the next aisle that I heard furious whispering from the group of stunned women.

"I WOULD'VE LOVED TO be there," Archie chuckled as I recounted the story to him half an hour later. "The nosy cows, I don't suppose you remember their names, from school?"

"Nope, sorry. They weren't the gorgeous ones you used to swoon over," I regretted the words as soon as they left my mouth. "I mean not the ones who used to swoon over you. You had better taste than that lot," I covered up my error, though a quick look at his face told me he knew what I'd said and what I'd meant.

It was complicated. Just because I didn't want to have a relationship with Archie, back then, it didn't mean I'd be happy if he went on a date with anyone else. Best friends, then, and now. I didn't understand social etiquette. Hidden deep in the mind of my mind, was the thought, that I should have agreed to the relationship we both wanted, but were too scared to try.

I was an annoying teen best friend. Every time he went out with a girl I found fault with her. Great friend that he was, he always listened to me. Just another thing I could wallow in regret about, if I chose to let it. If he found a nice girl now, and settled down, I'd be a little sad, but pleased for Archie. He deserved the best.

"Penny for your thoughts?" Archie's voice broke through my thoughts.

"Honestly? I was thinking about all the times you've had my back, and what a crap friend I've been. If you ever bring this up again though, I'll deny it." I gave my friend a quick hug, something else I rarely did. He hugged me back. It was I who eventually broke the connection. "So, jigsaw puzzle dinner?" I waved my arm at the bowls of food laid out on the table.

Archie chuckled, giving me a cheeky side-eye. "Of course, I'm looking forward to it."

AS I PULLED THE COVERS up, hours after Archie left, I contemplated my next move. After the bank reveals Margo's secrets, I could just leave town. Run from here and never return. The only reason I returned after I lost Leo, was because I thought West Haven would be safe, welcoming, a place to heal, regroup, and search for Leo.

Once it was clear my parents would be of no support, Archie's friendship and support became my only reason for staying in town. Honestly, back then, I was in no fit state to make decisions and wouldn't have known where to move to. My rental cottage meant I had somewhere to hide, heal, rant, cry and ride the emotional grief rollercoaster. With the library job, and Eve, I began to rebuild some semblance of normal. Building a life where I could eventually bring Leo home to.

Reality was a little different. The more I searched, the more Brandon's minions made life difficult. Having Archie, Eve, the cottage and my job – were they enough for me to stay, or should I run? Lose myself in the big city, somewhere that no one knows or cares about Scarlett Nightly. Where no one is hiding, ready to yell obscenities because big bad wolf Brandon tells them to.

Nettie's comments had cut deeper than I wanted to admit. If I left, Archie could finally get on with his life. The life he deserved.

"Disappearing into the anonymity sounds tantalisingly tempting," I told the silence in my room. Would Eve give me a reference and help me find another job? One that paid as well as the library, without me having to gain any formal qualifications.

I wriggled under the covers, pretending I was snuggling with Leo. As much as it hurt, talking aloud eased the pain, a little. *I do love the job with Eve, and I'm excited about the chance to plan and organise the Book Week parade. That's a few months away, it's only May now. Mother's Day. I wished I'd been closer to my own mum. She wasn't a cuddly, 'there there' parent. I'd like to think I would be different, kinder, more attentive...I hope I have the opportunity to find out one day.*

I wondered about my mother. What was her childhood like? Relationships and experiences mould us as we grow and adapt to our circumstances. My melt down taught me that. Where did my anxiety come from? Would Leo exhibit signs of anxiety? Will he be a different child with Brandon, than he would be with me?

The chance to be your mother, to be with you every day, to teach, guide, love, protect you, would be amazing. I'll never give up dreaming, planning, taking small steps to make it happen. Not a day goes by where I don't think of you, love you, hope you're safe, well, happy, and loved...

If I was to continue to search for Leo, and Brandon, things like the threatening email, the vandalism, the rude comments would continue. I wasn't worried about me, but Eve and Archie didn't deserve vandalism, and bullying. I may be overacting. Was there a third option? Run away, stay, or...

Would Leo want his mother to run away? That little voice that spoke on behalf of my son asked.

He's much better off without me, retorted the louder, stronger voice. It was an internal struggle, and at ten past midnight on Wednesday I wasn't sure which one would win the argument.

IN A SIMILAR DREAM as previously the faceless ghouls that chased me yelled profanities at me. I turned and yelled back. Their stunned look faded to nothingness. I stumbled, as darkness fell. I woke in panic, stuck in the bottom of a hole so dark in couldn't make out the shape of my hand in front of me. I screamed and woke myself up. It took a few seconds to realise I was safe, in my own bed and not stuck in a hole. Sweat poured off my body as I took control, one breath at a time.

One step at a time I showered, dressed and packed my leather handbag. I'd spent more on the bag than I normally spent in a month, as a present for myself for healing enough to start job hunting. It easily fit my laptop, my lunchbox, and drink bottle, which was a bonus. All in one bag with a free hand for groceries or opening the door.

While I'd not been keen to apply for unemployment benefits, after Leo, my doctor had convinced me I needed somewhere to live and food to eat while I healed. She'd been right of course. I'd saved enough for the handbag and formal work clothes, by the time I won the library job.

The lack of milk in my fridge didn't faze me and had nothing to do with money. *"I'm not keen on going back to the supermarket, though I can't live on Archie's café food, as yummy as it is,"* I told Leo's picture. If I moved somewhere else, I could buy groceries without worrying about bumping into mean, nosy, busy bodies, or people who knew my family. As tempting as that was, did I really want to start again?

A sharp rap at the door interrupted my thoughts. I unlocked the bolt and tentatively pulled open the wooden door. Archie stood on the other side of the still locked screen door, holding a large takeaway mug and a brown paper bag. "I noticed a severe lack of food and drink items in your fridge last night. I figured you wouldn't want to go to the supermarket before work."

"Or after work," I muttered. "Thank you so much!" I opened the door and relieved him of the offerings. "Are you coming in?" I already knew the answer, but the least I could do was ask, seeing as he delivered my breakfast.

"Nah, Pippa's minding the café, and she'll have to get to school soon. I've got wraps on as the lunch special if you want to call in. Your creativity with last night's dinner inspired me," he added with a wink. "Have a great day. Hey, you'll have to come past the café at lunch, to tell me what's in the deposit box."

Goose bumps ran up my arms at the mention of the mystery waiting for me at the bank. I tucked my socked feet into my black shoes. Instinct told me to take my laptop to work, something I didn't normally do. I slipped it into my brown leather bag. I kissed Leo's photo goodbye, leaving it on the kitchen bench so I'd see him as soon as I opened my door after work.

"You're bright and early this morning," Eve greeted me with a smile, as we arrived at the library's back door at the same time. Her long black dress suited her; the black ribbon in her hair adding that touch of elegance I'd never been able to achieve. She held open the heavy navy door for me.

"I thought I'd get in early, seeing as I have that appointment at 10am. I love your outfit by the way," I smiled at my boss. In another life, we could be friends, we shared the same love of books, food, and movies. Maybe one day, when I got my life sorted out.

"I found the dress at the local second-hand shop. It has some terrific bargains; I rarely bother with other dress shops. There are some shirts and dress skirts I think you'd like." Eve followed me to the little kitchen area. She unzipped her bag, putting her lunchbox in the fridge. "No sandwiches today?"

I shook my head. "I need to buy groceries. Archie offered to make me lunch if I call in after my appointment. I'll eat back here though. Do you have any afternoon meetings?"

"Only with you," she smiled. "We've got the official go ahead to plan our Book Week project. Bring your ideas with you when we meet after lunch. We'll sit out at one of the desks, so we're available can help customers while we brainstorm." Eve led the way to the front counter. "Are you good to look after the front counter, until your appointment? I want to get stuck into the storage area; it needs a good tidy up."

"Of course. It'll give me a chance to jot down some ideas myself. I knew there was a reason why I brought my laptop to work. Typing is so much faster than writing." I smiled, as ideas for Book Week activities swirled around in my head.

By the time I opened the doors at 9am I'd written two pages of Book Week activities. I helped a few of our regulars find their next reads. A couple of mums brought their children in to choose books and a toy to borrow. I nearly missed Nettie, as she slunk in behind Mr and Mrs Potts. Nettie had an old, tatty straw hat over her curly black hair. She was a few inches shorter than the Potts, a retired couple who came in every day to read the newspaper, Nettie shuffled along to the back row of shelves.

As I followed her, I saw her hold her mobile phone in front of her. "What are you doing?" I hoped my voice was firm enough to startle her.

She swung around to face me. "You can't stop me," the venom in her voice hit me like a slap on my face. "It's a free country."

"I can ask you not to film in the library, and to speak quietly, and respectfully." I stood my ground. I heard movement as Eve exited the storeroom and joined me. She didn't speak, neither did Nettie. For a few seconds Eve and I held Nettie's unblinking stare.

Eventually Nettie shoved her phone into the floral handbag draped over her arm. "Hmph, well, we'll see about that," she said haughtily, deliberately pushing into me as she moved past. She glanced at Eve, frowned and muttered to herself she exited the building.

Chapter Seven

I expected a room like in the movies, with safety deposit boxes lining the walls. Instead, Mr Wells, the bank manager led me into a spare office. On the large wooden table in the middle of the room sat a black metal box. "I'll leave you to it," he nodded. "Take all the time you need. Margo's instructions were clear, that the entire contents of the box are yours. You can continue to store the items here or take them with you."

Once the bank manager left the room, I unlocked the box. My stomach tied in knots; I had to force myself to breathe. The only item inside the metal container was a manilla folder. I opened it gingerly, as if the contents were going to bite. The first few pages of information appeared to be copies from a book about the Watson family. It confirmed Brandon Kelly was Gerald Watson's stepson and further confirmed the Kellys appeared in the Watson family tree by marriage, about one hundred years ago. Another branch of the family tree recorded the Nightlys as distant relatives, around the same time.

Copies of newspaper clippings followed. Forty years ago, Brandon's mother and mine entered in a showgirl pageant. My mother won by five votes. Brandon's mother stormed out of the pavilion. In another article my father was listed as one of the recipients of a scholarship to study medicine. A handwritten note indicated Brandon's father had also applied and missed out. My parents were dubbed belles of the ball, the photograph in the paper showing them smiling while behind them, a couple I now recognised as Brandon's parents, scowled.

Could Brandon have deliberately sought me out, to take advantage, get me pregnant and steal my child, as payback for what happened to his family? It seemed to be implied by the documents in front of me. I searched the contents of the box for a handwritten note or something in Margo's own hand. Something to confirm I was correctly interrupting the documents in front of me. There was a notebook, but the handwriting made no sense. Could it be shorthand? Aware of the time, I gathered the contents of the box into my bag, thanking Mr Wells on my way out of the bank.

I FELT STRANGELY CALM as I made my way to the café. Customers chatted as they waited for their morning tea. I leant in close to Archie and whispered, "It's big, we can't talk here." I knew I sounded a little like I belonged in a mystery novel. I couldn't think of another way to explain that the information I found was important and may solve part of the mystery of Brandon's behaviour. My head was spinning with questions.

Archie raised an eyebrow. The 11am morning tea, pre-lunch crowd were in full force. I noted Nettie was absent, though I almost swung around to see if she was lurking behind me somewhere. "Okay, it's probably better we wait until later to talk, it's crazy in here." He leant over to the back bench and picked up a couple of brown bags. "A salad wrap, muffins, and here," he passed me a large takeaway mug, "A mocha." He waved away the twenty dollar note I tried to hand to him. "Just get some groceries before I turn up for a full debrief. I'll be exhausted if these crowds continue all day," he added.

I sighed theatrically. "I guess, the least I can do, is make sure there's ample food and drink at my house, seeing as you've been feeding me, making sure I don't fade away to nothing." I held my hand to my forehead in jest.

My friend waggled his finger at me, "Don't you order the groceries to be delivered. Go in person and choose the food and drink you want, enough for at least a week," he pretending to sound stern.

I laughed, as I waved and left him to the growing line of customers. The library was quiet by comparison. There were a few students in the research section, and a couple of oldies reading the paper. A mother and her three children were reading quietly in the children's section.

Eve stood shelving books, with a line of sight to the front counter. "If you want a break, I'll just drop my lunch in the kitchen and watch the front counter," I whispered.

"Thanks Scarlett, I'm looking forward to our Book Week planning after lunch." As I watched Eve disappear into the kitchen, I realised I was also looking forward to it too. Maybe it would all work out, and I'd stay here, in West Haven, and organise the Book Week festivities. I let my mind wander, with thoughts of a future in the library, feeling like I belonged somewhere. I ended up sitting at the counter to eat my lunch. I pushed all thoughts of the mystery out of my mind and focused on the Book Week plan.

AFTER A PRODUCTIVE afternoon planning session, a trip to the supermarket didn't feel as daunting. I held my head high, and moved from aisle to aisle, pushing the trolley as I collected items for my kitchen. *One step at a time,* I told myself. I could get myself set up, at home and at work, make a go of things, here. Then I could get Leo to come home. I found myself smiling as I chose fresh fruit and vegetables, and some treats from the bakery section. Once I'd collected new stock of the staples I'd run out of, and enough food for meals for the next few days, I was almost at the checkout.

"Good afternoon how has your day been?" asked the young lass with her hair tied high in a ponytail as she swiped my items through.

"I've had a lovely day thank you," I answered honestly, surprised to hear the smile in my voice.

"Yoohoo, Scarlett! It's great to see you out and about," Linda, a friend of my mother's waved from the checkout beside me. "Did you know your parents are both away? Your mother won another award, and your father has organised another school to be built."

I couldn't tell if she was being innocently nice, or rubbing it in. Maybe she didn't know about my less than positive relationship with my parents. I nodded and smiled in return, as someone behind me harrumphed. I turned to see why. I didn't recognise the person, but they were frowning at me. Or, maybe, they were just frowning. People were entitled to down time at the supermarket, that in limbo period between work and home. A good interlude to let go of any annoyances of the day, before heading home to family. I laughed at myself for being paranoid. They were probably impatient, anxious to get home.

Chapter Eight

I rarely wished I owned a car. Today though, it would have come in handy. I made a mental note to myself to not let the cupboards become so empty next time. I lugged the four full bags along the street: grateful I'd chosen reusable material bags and not the thinner paper ones. I sat the groceries on the front step as I unlocked the door.

"Oh, my goodness!" I dropped my keys, as I surveyed the mess that greeted me. I hadn't had the opportunity to collect a lot of things since returning home. What little amount I owned were strewn about the room. Scrawled in thick black pen, across the green laminated kitchen bench was the word LEAVE. I found it difficult to swallow, as I remembered I'd left Leo's photo on the kitchen bench as I left home this morning.

Finding an inner calm I didn't know I possessed, I bent to pick up the papers, books, and candles off the floor. Remembering the groceries, I brought them inside and packed them away. Taking back control one item at a time. *I will not be run out of town.* I told myself. I have as much right to be here as anyone else.

"Whoa, you've had a clean-up in here? I mean, your place is always tidier than mine, but it looks like you've had a spring clean. And you've got the groceries," he added, noticing the table set for dinner. "Good job." My best friend tried to boost my confidence every chance he got. I exhaled the breath I'd gulped, as Archie's entering my house startled me. He peered a little more closely at me. "Are you okay? I didn't mean to surprise you."

"I know that. I'm a little jumpy this afternoon, that's all. I've got us garlic bread and a mixed salad for dinner, with chocolate ice cream for dessert. If you want to take a seat." I slowed my breathing, working out how best to fill Archie in on the latest events. "How's your day been?"

"Same old thing," he smiled, sliding into one of the chairs at the little round wooden table. "Customers, coffee, cakes...I love it." He filled the two glasses with the ginger beer I'd placed on the table. "Are you going to fill me in on what happened at the bank?"

"Oh that, yes, okay." It felt like the bank visit was days ago, not merely a few hours. So much happened in such a short time. I took the garlic bread out of the oven, placing it on the table next to the salad. "Nettie visited the library early this morning, trying to cause a mischief. I stood up to her and asked her to leave." I felt the adrenaline as it sped along my body. "This is where it gets interesting. At the bank I discovered that Margo left me a lot of information to read through, but basically my parents, and Brandon's have been enemies for years. The Kellys blame my family for everything that's gone wrong, big and small. I'll have to re-read it in detail, but now it looks like Brandon planned our meeting and ultimately to steal Leo from me." I paused, as I chewed a piece of garlic bread. "Speaking of Leo, do you remember if I gave you a copy of his photo? Someone broke in here today, left me a crude message, messed up the place, and stole the only photo I had." My voice broke a little at the end, I shook my head, clearing away the melancholy.

"Are you sure you're okay?" Archie touched my arm briefly. Long enough for warm tingles to shoot along my arms. Did he feel it too? Was I reading too much into a simple gesture?

I considered my response. "Surprisingly, yes. Last night, or rather early this morning, I almost talked myself into leaving town. To disappear back into a big city, where no one knows me. Leaving you, Eve and the job would be difficult, part of me loves it here, and I can see a future for myself, and Leo, in this town. I don't know..." I my heart sunk at the look on Archie's face. "To be honest, it still may be an option, but only if things don't go according to plan. I don't want you or Eve in danger." I held up my hand, "Please don't say anything, it would only be a last resort. I want to focus on the information Margo left for me." I pulled the papers out of my handbag, relieved I'd not left my laptop at home this morning. If only I'd thought to take Leo's photo as well.

Archie piled a scoop of salad onto both our plates. "This information, what are you hoping to find? Apart from an address for Brandon and Leo."

"Thanks." I picked up a handful of green leaves. "The more I can understand about the feud between the Kellys and the Nightlys, the more prepared I'll be when I find them. Feud may be too strong a word, I don't think my parents would consider the events the same way Brandon's parents did. They seemed to take it personally, when my parents achieved some of the goals his parents aimed for. Please, read it for yourself, you'll see what I mean."

As he munched on a handful of salad, Archie skimmed through the pages. "It's weird that neither of us heard of Brandon when he lived here. I don't remember either of our parents mentioning anyone with the name Kelly."

"I was thinking the same. The Watson family tree is massive. Kelly and Nightly both appear on there, many years ago. Not that I think I'm directly related to the Watsons or Kellys." I shuddered involuntarily. "I don't suppose you know anyone who can read shorthand." I placed the notebook on the top of the pile of papers. "I'm hoping this will contain an address, or some clue to where I can find Leo."

Archie raised his eyebrows. "I hope there are no Scotts in that family tree," He said hopefully. "Shorthand, I think a few of the girls from school can read shorthand, but I can't guarantee they'd decipher it correctly. Or keep what they learn to themselves."

"Good point," I agreed. "I can probably find a key to how to read it on the internet, or maybe at the library. Now let's have some ice cream before I beat you at cards."

The clock ticked over to 10pm by the time we finished playing cards. "I finally beat you!" I held my fist up triumphantly.

"Hmm, well, a re-match is in order, tomorrow." He grinned, hugging me as I walked with him to the door. The gesture caught me by surprise. He chuckled as I stared at him speechless, after I hugged him back. It felt the safest thing in the world. Except we both swore to remain 'just friends.'

I made sure the doors and windows were locked after Archie left. Too wired to sleep. What did I want to do with Margo's information? I flicked through the documents.

My mobile beeped, indicating an email in my inbox. I opened my laptop, bringing the inbox up on the screen. A video icon blinked up on my email. My body jumped involuntarily as I saw the face on the screen.

Brandon's face sneered at me. His dark brown eyes, short brown hair, and olive skin. The features I'd once found attractive made me cringe. *You'll never find us so you may as well stop trying. You know you won't succeed. Go away, we don't want you. Leo doesn't want you.*

I closed the video, and slammed the lid down, with shaking hands. My heart thumping so loud in my chest I couldn't think straight. How could I ever have thought I loved that horrible man? The snide comments, the bullying, the verbal abuse. Yuck! I stood so quickly I knocked the chair over.

Part of my wanted to run and hide. Another part of me wanted to fight. Which half would win? I yawned. There wasn't much chance of sleeping. I glanced at the books on my shelf. Maybe I could read, totally distract myself. One of the techniques I'd learnt to quell anxious thoughts – to choose something totally unrelated to focus on.

A couple of hours, and a hundred pages later, I decided to try to get some sleep. I didn't expect to quieten my brain enough to doze off.

Each time I closed my eyes I saw his face. Brandon's. Sneering at me. Telling me I was useless. That no one would ever love me.

By 5am I gave up on sleeping and returned to the book. At 6am I jumped in the shower and dressed for work. I gulped down a coffee. In hindsight an herbal tea may have been wiser. My body was buzzing with nervous energy.

I rarely jog but today seemed like a good day to start. As my feet thumped on the footpath I concentrated on my breathing. Soon I slowed to a brisk walk. Should I tell Archie about the video? Show him the video? If I didn't and he found out later – he'd be mad, and I wouldn't blame him. I marched home, and collected my bag, making sure my laptop was in it. Only after I left, did I realise I had a kitchen full of food, but I hadn't made lunch, or even packed my drink bottle.

Archie waved as I opened the café door. "I didn't expect to see you this early," he smiled. "Not that I mind, of course. Coffee?"

"Yes please," I replied, the earlier caffeine buzz faded, I needed a recharge. I plonked my bottom on one of the stools at the counter.

"What's up?" Archie asked as he passed me a large takeaway cup. "As much as I love your company, I know you didn't just drop in."

"Don't be mad," I hesitated, waiting for the Archie look. That sideways stare he gave me when I acted stubborn and he wanted to protect me. "I received another email, a video, from Brandon." I passed my laptop to Archie to see for himself, cringing as I heard the venomous words again.

He closed the laptop, smacking his hand on the metal lid. "The hide of him!"

I placed my hand on my best friend's arm. "He's a horrible nasty man. What he says still hurts, but I'm angry, and determined to find him. To bring Leo home." I leant over and gave him a quick hug. "I told you, because I didn't want to keep secrets from you. Please don't stay angry. I need calm Archie, to help me."

Just then a crowd of coffee lovers arrived. I recognised them as regulars. Archie glanced at them and looked back at me. "I'm okay, if you are." He gave me that Archie stare.

"Surprisingly, I am calmer than I expected to be." It was the truth. I'd a sense of calm I didn't expect. I wasn't going to let Brandon win.

Chapter Nine

I didn't recognise the policeman who stood at the counter. My intuition told me he was at the library to speak to me. The look of sadness on Eve's face confirmed my worst fears. Something was very wrong.

"Scarlett Nightly?" The policeman asked as I approached.

I nodded, not able to find my voice.

Eve moved towards me. "This is Officer Dean," she said softly.

"Can we sit down?" as the policeman said those ominous words I looked to Eve for confirmation. I let them lead me to the closest seats. A couple of semi comfortable chairs by a low table. Eve sat next to me and squeezed my hand as the Officer Dean spoke quietly, "I'm sorry to have to inform you, that your parents were both killed in an accident late last night."

When my mouth opened, my voice sounded odd, like I was speaking through fog. "You must be mistaken. Someone told me my parents were out of town." I couldn't remember who, a friend of my mother's, at the supermarket.

The man in uniform nodded solemnly. "They were in Demark. Travelling on a train. I don't have any other details. I'm sorry." He looked genuinely sorry for my loss. "I know a little about what happens when Australians die overseas." The policeman continued, "The official process is to organise their funerals locally in Denmark, and have their remains returned to Australia. I have the contact details of someone who can assist you."

As he spoke, I tried to feel, something, anything. Should I be crying? Should I feel sad, devastated, that both my parents were dead? I'd used up all my tears when they ignored me on my return to West Haven. I felt nothing as my brain started ticking off a macabre to do list – funeral, cremation, return ashes, sell house, making the assumption that as their only child I would be their next of kin. I tried to concentrate on the words being spoken by the middle-aged policeman in front of me. "If you need anything at all, please don't hesitate to contact the station."

Eve squeezed my hand. I focused on her as I heard her speak. "Thank you, Officer Dean. That's a lot of information to process. As I understand, from what you've just said, that the first thing Scarlett needs to do is talk to the relevant person in Denmark."

Officer Dean handed me a piece of paper. "Yes, here are the contact details. Try ringing first and follow up with an email. Once again, please accept my deepest sympathies. Tom and Dora were wonderful people. Terrific assets to our community." He shook my hand, awkwardly, as we stood.

"Thank you," I said equally stiffly, my head spinning. I let Eve walk the policeman to the door, thankful that there were only a couple of patrons in the library, neither of whom seemed the slightest bit interested in why there was a law enforcement officer in the library.

"Let's get you a nice cup of tea," Eve suggested as she returned to my side.

"Do you mind if I have a coffee, and if I keep working on the plans for Book Week?" I asked quietly. "I know I haven't told you a lot about my past, but when I returned to West Haven, needing support, neither of my parents were interested in helping me. I'll bring them home, and I'll probably shed some tears, but I'd like to keep working on the Book Week project, if that's okay."

Eve looked like she wanted to hug me but changed her mind. "Whatever you need. I'll bring you a coffee out here. Do you want me to contact anyone for you?"

I shook my head, "No thank you, and yes a coffee would be nice." I pulled out my laptop, where I'd taken notes and started some project documents. I pulled up a new word document and started a new list titled *Parents*.

"Did your parents have any other family?" Eve asked, as she placed a mug of steaming coffee in front of me. She sat opposite me with a cup of tea.

"Dad has a brother, Mum has a sister, both of whom have houses locally but live overseas. At least that's my recollection. I suppose I should let them know." I typed *let people know* on my new page, under *organise funeral*. "Do I let people know, locally? How? Is it still by placing their death notice in the paper?"

Before Eve could answer my phone vibrated, indicating an incoming call. I didn't recognise the number. "Hello, Scarlett Nightly speaking. Hello, yes, oh I see, okay, thank you." I hung up the call and placed my mobile on the table. "That was odd. Mr Sinclair, the solicitor, rang to tell me my aunt and uncle were appointed joint executors of my parents' estate. They, through Sinclair Attorneys, will organise everything, from my parents' funeral, to bringing their ashes home, the death notice, and the memorial service. I'll be advised when they have the reading of the will. My services are not required."

Eve sat up straight, making her even taller than she normally appeared. "That's outrageous! Family is important. Take it from someone who was an orphan, adopted at the age of five. If you need anything, anything at all, you let me know," she said fiercely.

I couldn't help smiling, despite the drama of the morning, and the odd events over the last few days. "Thank you, Eve. Honestly, right now, if we can get the Book Week project nutted out, and then maybe, if we have time later in the week, I have a mystery I'd like your help in solving."

Eve gave me a puzzled look and shrugged. "Okay, sounds like a plan, and intriguing. I love a good mystery. Do you need to take a moment, talk to Archie, or anything, before you show me your Book Week ideas?"

Did I need a moment? Probably, but the problem was if I took any time to stop and process the news delivered by Officer Dean, I'd fall apart and end up curled under a blanket on the lounge watching television. Not ending up in a blubbering heap after seeing Brandon was a huge step for me.

Should I talk to Archie? Yes, but I dare not speak the words aloud. I couldn't share with him what the police told me, or about the weird telephone call from the solicitors. He'd want to look after me, and I'd end up a bawling mess unable to leave my house.

"I need to feel useful," I told Eve. "Too many people have told me that I'm not a productive member of society. You and Archie are the only two who see past my anxiety and acknowledge me as a person." I couldn't find the right words. "I need to tell Archie, but I need to not fall apart. There's too much at stake." I stopped speaking, as my voice wobbled. I swallowed the lump in my throat. "If you don't mind, I'll just work on the project."

Eve nodded. "I'll grab us some brain food."

I SET UP MY LAPTOP where I could see the front door. Our Book Week activities were something positive I could focus on. As I made notes I noticed a teenager, his face masked by a bike helmet, drop an envelope on the front counter. I walked over to see what it was. The small white envelope had my name written on it, in fancy handwritten flowery font.

Carefully peeling open the envelope, I found a tarot card – *the Queen of Wands*. On the back of the card were written the words – confidence, strength, courage, and self-awareness. A second look at the envelope revealed no clues as to the sender. "It's not the strangest thing to happen to me today," I muttered aloud. During my university days I'd visited a psychic to have my tarot cards read. I even had my own set, tucked away somewhere in the bottom of a cupboard.

"What have you got there, dearie?" Mrs Mac leant over the counter as I held the card. Distracted with the envelope, I'd not noticed her entering the library. "Oh, a tarot card, how fascinating. I used to read cards, years ago. *The Queen of Wands* is a good one. It's about believing in yourself, confidence, and trust." She handed me a pile of books. "I've finished these, can I leave them with you, while I go and hunt for some more?"

"You sure can. Bring over the books you'd like to borrow, and I'll run them through the system for you." I smiled at my old art teacher. She wore a long flowing multi-coloured kaftan. Not as tall as Eve, she stood a little taller than my 165cm. It didn't surprise me she knew about tarot; the other kids called her 'hippy dippy'. I tucked the card into the pocket of my jeans and busied myself with returning Mrs Mac's books on the system.

Life as a teenager was a lot simpler. Before university, before Brandon. My parents were always busy. I managed their high expectations of me to excel at every subject. I found it easy to study, even exams didn't faze me too much. Facts and figures were easier than relationships. I chose to stay home and read, when most of my peers were out partying. When I moved to the city, to university, it all started to go awry.

"Are you okay Scarlett?" Eve asked as she returned, with takeaway mugs and paper bags with food. I didn't ask her if she'd spoken to Archie. I couldn't think about the news from Officer Dean, not yet.

"Yes. Thank you for getting us lunch," I replied as she put the goodies on the desk where I'd been working. "I was just thinking about school. That's my art teacher in the romance section. I was the typical nerd at school; I didn't mind not having a lot of friends. I liked to study. That changed when I started at university. Discovering the bright lights of the city, I got a little distracted, I didn't like the subjects I was studying." I held up *the Queen of Wands*. "Changing the subject, I don't suppose you know anything about tarot? This arrived in an envelope with my name on it."

Eve held out her hand for the card, turning it over in her hand. "These always scared me. I had a bad experience with a Ouija board as a teenager." She handed it back to me. "Do you think you should talk to the police about this?"

I looked at the card. It didn't feel dangerous, or part of anything sinister. Someone's idea of a prank maybe? Not Brandon, as it appeared to offer a positive message for me. "I'll think about talking to Officer Dean," I promised Eve, as Mrs Mac returned to the counter. "Did you find the books you were looking for?"

"Yes dear, I did. I love the new trend, of cozy mystery books. Reminds me of Miss Marple. I have five books here. I noticed you have a couple of books on tarot on the shelves, if you're interested in knowing more about that card," she added, with a smile.

As Mrs Mac left the building, I mused aloud that maybe I'd find my tarot cards when I returned home and ask the universe to reveal some answers.

BY THE MIDDLE OF THE afternoon, Eve and I were happy with our preparations for Book Week. "Why don't you go see Archie, or go home and rest," Eve suggested.

I knew I couldn't put it off any longer. "I'll talk to Archie, and I'll bring us back coffees, if that's okay. I'm not ready to go home yet."

The café was bustling with the normal after school traffic. I hopped onto a vacant stool at the counter. My best friend watched me approach, keeping one eye on the chocolate thick shake he was creating. "Eve told me," he said quietly, as he poured the thick mixture into a plastic takeaway glass. "She explained you needed to focus on work. Are you okay?"

I nodded. "Thanks for the salad sandwiches, choc chip banana muffins and mochas. We achieved a lot, planning our Book Week activities."

Archie moved to the coffee machine and scooped the coffee into the metal gadget to make the next order. He placed half a dozen cinnamon donuts into a bag. "Carrie was in here mouthing off. I try not to listen to her gossip, but she mentioned your parents."

The lump in my throat returned. I wanted to hug my best friend. "I'm sorry you had to hear it from Carrie. I just couldn't..."

"I know," he said softly, briefly patting my hand. "Eve didn't tell me all the details. Carrie was full of them." He handed two takeaway cups to the waiting customer. With no one else waiting to be served, he moved closer to where I sat and whispered. "She said they died overseas in a freak train accident. That your aunt and uncle are executors and you've been told not to have anything to do with bringing them home."

"Yep, that's pretty much it in a nutshell. I thought my head was going to explode. I couldn't talk to you or think about it. You know how I deal with all the big stuff – either fall apart totally, or hyperfocus on work. It's not like my parents and I were close, especially after Leo. I cried so much when I returned home. When I realised they weren't there for me. I lost them then." I knew Archie would understand.

Before he could answer a group of teenagers walked into the café. It was only on my way back to the library, after I'd promised to meet him after work, that I remembered about the coffees.

Chapter Ten

Officer Dean said the explosion was the result of my leaving the gas stove top on by accident. I rarely used the stove top in my little cottage and only used the oven half a dozen times. The microwave, kettle, toaster, and an electric wok Archie bought me were the only tools I used for cooking. The policeman looked like he might cry, as he told me. "The damage caused by water and as the firemen doused the fire destroyed anything not damaged by the initial blast. I'm sorry, but I doubt that anything can be salvaged."

The apologetic policeman delivered the news to me at the library, just before closing. Eve offered me a room at her place, but I politely declined. As much as I liked my boss, my independence kicked in. "Thanks Eve, but I'll book into the motel down the road."

Eve eyed me worriedly. "Go to the café, talk to Archie, please Scarlett. I'm worried about you. I know it's none of my business, but it's a lot for anyone to take in."

"I will. I consider you a friend, as well as my boss. I won't stay at Archie's either. It's a stubborn thing. I will be okay," I said the words to make her feel better. I didn't know how I felt. Losing my parents and my home in less than twenty-four hours.

I clutched my handbag as I headed to the café. A stray tear ran down my cheek as I realised these were the only items I owned. I patted my bag, checking my laptop was inside. Earlier Archie reminded me I'd kept a copy of Leo's photo on it.

"I briefly considered staying at my parents' house," I told him over my mocha and chocolate brownie. Archie knew I was coming, thanks to the local gossip vine. Carrie had spread news of the events at my house before I had a chance to tell my best friend. An explosion in town was newsworthy by anyone's standards. He closed the café a little early, politely asking the last few customers to leave, as soon as I arrived.

"You'll stay at mine, until you can sort something out." Archie's eyes searched mine.

I smiled, a watery grin. "I'm okay, honestly. At least more okay than I thought I'd be, knowing that my parents are dead, I'm not to be involved in bringing them home, or sorting out their estate, and now I don't have anywhere to live." I thought about what to say next as I ate some of the brownie. "Thanks for your offer, but I'm going to stay at the Elm Tree Motel." I held my hand up. "Before you argue, I'm a little worried about something happening to you, if I stay at yours. Call me paranoid, or cautious. I declined Eve's offer of a room for the same reason." It had crossed my mind, that someone was targeting me. I couldn't bear the thought of harm coming to Archie or Eve.

"Can I at least buy you some dinner?" Archie's eyes filled with tears. I hated that I was causing him more pain, but my intuition told me the incidents were linked. I hoped to find the key amongst the information in the folder from Margo. That folder was safely in my bag. I wasn't letting it leave my sight.

"I'd like that. Can we make it a late dinner? I want to see if I can pick up some items at the shop." Our local supermarket stocked lots of useful bits and pieces, including underwear, and other basic clothing items.

"Pizza? Around 7pm." I could tell he was trying his best not to cry. I felt hot tears threatening to run down my face.

"Perfect!" I finished my mocha. "Do you want me to pick anything up for you?"

"Not that I can think of," Archie replied. He wrapped his arms around me as we both left the table. "Be careful," he said, his voice taking on a serious tone. "I'm not saying you're right, about being targeted, but just in case, take a taxi to the motel. Please."

"I will," I promised. Archie was more worried than I, but then my adrenaline had overridden my fear.

I SAW THE IRONY IN my second trip to the supermarket in as many days. All those groceries I bought twenty-four hours ago, destroyed. *Move forward, everything will be okay.* I told myself as I headed to the non-food aisles. Toiletries, underwear, a couple of t-shirts, a pair of summery pants, and purple pyjamas. I'd need to duck into one of the clothes shops in the morning, to grab some more items, but at least I had a change of clothes now. On the way to the registers, I picked up a bag of chocolates, and raspberries, and a couple of bottles of water.

Did I imagine the whispered comments of the other customers in the aisles? Losing my parents and my home in less than twenty-four hours was extraordinarily unusual. I couldn't blame people if they chose to talk about what'd happened to me. In a small town like West Haven there would always be drama to talk about.

Were the events related? Could Brandon be targeting me, and not just threatening me? Did the information from the safety deposit box pose a threat to him? Apart from Nettie, there must be others in town in contact with Brandon. Were they spying on me? Who could he brainwash enough to cause the fire? I knew only too well how coercive he could be. Rather than overthinking, it was time for action.

Luckily an taxi waited in the taxi rank just outside the supermarket, otherwise I'd have probably just walked the few hundred metres to the motel. I piled my bags into the back seat and hopped into the front. "Where to?" the man's voice sounded mildly irritated.

"The Elm Tree Motel please," I told him. Something about the man seemed familiar. Did I go to school with him? I'd not paid much attention to boys at school to be honest. His thinning brown hair tied in a straggly ponytail at the back, reminded me of someone, I just couldn't put my finger on who.

"Right," he said gruffly, as he swung the vehicle out into the road. My stomach flip flopped as he threw the taxi around roughly. I wished I'd walked. Walking would be safer, even in the dark. I didn't feel comfortable in the car with this maniac driver.

Archie gave a thumbs up to the driver and laughed as I exited the taxi. "You didn't recognise Greyson, did you? He sat behind us in science class for three years at high school."

"Greyson who left school to travel the world with his parents?" I asked incredulously, remembering a tall lanky lad with thick glasses and long wavy brown hair.

"The same one. Taxi driving pays for his yearly trip overseas. Did he scare you with his driving?" he chuckled.

"Only a little," I retorted, feeling braver now I was standing on firm ground.

A middle-aged woman, her blonde hair in a bun, wearing jeans and a long-sleeved navy shirt, opened the door to reception. "Scarlett Nightly?" she asked as she joined us. "I'm Gemma, I just wanted to say I'm sorry, I can't imagine how you must be feeling..." her voice trailed off. She managed a little smile as she nodded to Archie. Everyone knew and loved Archie, and his ability to make amazing coffee and mouth-watering sweet treats. She returned her gaze to me. "I've put you in room 201, our biggest room. I'll only charge you fifty dollars a night, which is the cost of cleaning and servicing the room. It's available for the next seven days. After that we can look at other options if you still need somewhere." She handed me a key on a large square plastic tag. "In the room you'll find the Wi-Fi code, and a breakfast menu. If you want to order breakfast for tomorrow just pop the completed breakfast form outside your door by 8pm. Any questions, pick up the phone and dial nine." She eyed the pizza boxes, the bags of food Archie held, and the bags I'd shifted to one hand, holding the key in the other. "I'll let you get settled."

"Thanks Gemma," I replied, as she turned to re-enter the reception area.

Archie pointed to the room at the far end of the row of rooms on our right. "I may have stayed here a few times myself," he grinned as his cheeks flushed a shiny red colour.

"Do tell," I grinned back. A good looking, nice young man like Archie would be a catch for anyone. Women tended to flirt with him, and sometimes he flirted back. I knew he wasn't waiting for me to decide to live happily ever after with him. We both knew that was unlikely.

"I don't want to ruin your appetite," he quipped, holding the pizza boxes in the air. "Let's get this lot inside."

My stomach made a gurgling noise, reminding me I'd not eaten much over the course of the day.

Archie left after 9pm, making me promise to wait for him to drive me to work the next day. We'd eaten all the pizza, garlic bread, and gooey chocolate dessert without once referring to the events of the day. Instead, we found re-runs of an old comedy show on television and spent the best part of two hours laughing as we stuffed our faces with food.

After changing into my new pyjamas, I turned off the television and placed the Margo file as I was calling it, on the little table. Grateful for the larger room, which included a table and two chairs, as well as the bed and a little sofa, I didn't immediately feel claustrophobic.

By 11pm I'd read all the documents, made copious notes, and a plan. There were options, and Archie and Eve wouldn't like my decision. I weighed the pros and cons. I knew what I had to do.

As I lay in the dark anxiety and doubt crept in.

I don't want to stop searching for you Leo. Without my parents, or a home here, it'd be easy to crawl under the covers and hide. The thing is, I want to find you, to bring you home. For you to grow up here, with me, Archie, and Eve. Where people love you. I could give up, but I don't want to.

I'll mourn my parents, your grandparents, in my own way. I'm sad they didn't have a chance to get to know you. They were tough on me. Maybe I needed that tough love, to push through my anxiety and fear.

Tears streamed down my cheeks. I tasted their saltiness as they found my lips. Tears for my boy who was so far away. Tears for my parents, that I wouldn't have the chance to make peace. Tears for my little cottage. I did not leave the stove top on. It was arson. My hands formed fists as I thought about Brandon, deliberately targeting me.

I hated that Archie and Eve mightn't be safe. They were close to me. Would Brandon go so far as to hurt them? My decision, to move to the city, was the correct one. To leave West Haven behind, to keep them safe. Brandon wouldn't be able to find me. Whether I kept searching for him or curled up and let anxiety eat me. I could find him. Bring Leo home. Brandon wouldn't see me coming.

But what if...that little nagging voice of doubt ran through my dreams. Being chased by monsters with Brandon's face.

Chapter Eleven

Archie knocked on the door early. I opened the door, already dressed and ready for the day. I wasn't ready to tell him my decision yet. I knew he'd try and talk me out of it.

He embraced me, his emotion easy to read. I was just as exhausted and overwhelmed by the enormity of the events of the previous day. I returned the hug, neither of us wanting to release the other.

"Breakfast?" Archie asked quietly. "Whatever you want at the café." He held my arms, his eyes searching mine. Reluctantly, he released his hold.

I linked my arm through his, my handbag in my other hand. "I'd love that, thank you." I squeezed his arm. "You know I'm not ready to talk, but are you okay? I worry about you too, you know." I felt guilty, knowing my decision would hurt him. It was for his safety, and Eve's.

"As long as you are here, and doing okay, so am I," he responded cheerfully. I heard the quiver in his voice he tried so hard to hide.

I ARRIVED AT THE LIBRARY before Eve. Archie insisted on sending snacks and more coffee with me. He also made me promise to call in during the day. I think he half suspected I was going to run away and wanted to keep an eye on me.

A white envelope with my name on it, sat on top of the returned books when I emptied the book chute. It didn't surprise me that a tarot card greeted me. The card – *The World* signified all the opportunities open for me, if only I dared to dream. "Yeah, right," I muttered aloud, tucking the card into my bag. So much for getting out my tarot cards and reading the future. Replacing them sat way down the list, after finding and setting up a home, buying furniture, food, and new clothes. I looked down at the pale blue t-shirt with a smiling daisy emblazoned on it. The clothing choices at the supermarket were limited, but my casual top did make me smile.

Eve exited the kitchen carrying two bottles of orange juice. "I thought we could both do with some vitamin C. Before we attack the treats from Archie." She handed one bottle to me. "It doesn't look too bad," she said, noticing my appraisal of my shirt. "Have a look in the bag in the storeroom. I brought along a few clothes I thought you might like. Don't feel pressured, they'll go to the second-hand shop if you decide not to use them."

I nodded; not sure I trusted my voice not to break. Eve's generosity made what I needed to say, even more difficult. I loved Eve's taste in clothes. I considered choosing all the items in the bag, but if I was moving to the city that wouldn't be practical. I chose some floral dress shirts and a couple of trousers, one green and one maroon. Perfect to mix and match. I emerged from the storeroom in the green pants and a cream shirt and enveloped her in a hug. "Thank you," I whispered.

Once I drained the bottle of juice, I felt a little stronger. "Have you got a few moments?" Eve nodded as I led her to a table that let us talk and watch the front counter. "It's May now, Book Week is in three months, in August." I didn't wait for Eve to confirm, or I'd lose my nerve. "I need to take leave, I don't know how long for, but I want to be able to come back for Book Week. I need that to look forward to."

Eve's hazel eyes held my gaze. She reached out and held my hand but didn't speak.

"I want to explain, you deserve that. Apart from Archie, you're the only one who took a chance on me." I took a deep breath, exhaling slowly. "I don't suppose you've heard of a man called Brandon Kelly. His name's not important," I continued in a rush to get my story out before I chickened out. "I met him at university. I got pregnant and gave birth to a baby named Leo. Brandon stole him out of the hospital and took him away somewhere. I returned home, hoping my parents would help me find him. They didn't. I spent a year crying, the next year, feeling a little better, still too broken to do much except try to heal, then I eventually started looking for work." I felt tears running in little tracks down my cheek. "I had to stop trying to find Leo, until I healed, or I would've ended up locked away. For the first two years, Archie looked after me, he visited every day. He made sure I had food and slowly set me challenges. Making me do my own shopping, so that I left the house occasionally." I took another deep breath in, releasing it as I continued. "Anyway, when Margo Watson died, I overheard her brother talk about his stepson Brandon Kelly. In the box I received at the bank, Margo left me some clues to follow, and you know the rest. I think Brandon has people like Nettie, doing his bidding, trying to scare me." I shook my head as Eve opened her mouth to speak. "I'd be devastated if anything happened to you, or Archie. After yesterday I can't be sure you are both safe if I stay in town. I need to resolve this, one way or the other, but not in West Haven. I must go to the city, where no one knows me." I felt alternately energised and deflated. "I want to be able to return once it's over."

Eve looked at me. She took both my hands in hers. As she released them, she spoke. "Thank you, for trusting me enough to tell me your story. I've not heard of the man you mentioned, but I know the Watsons are a family who wield power and influence. Margo more so than any of the others. I can't begin to imagine what you've been through, what you're still going through. Take as much leave as you need. Your job will be here when you return. I don't like the idea of you being by yourself, but I understand why you must leave. If I can help from here, I'd like to."

"I don't suppose you know shorthand code?" I held up the notebook. "This is the part of the mystery I referred to before. I found it amongst the items Margo left me."

Eve took the notebook, flipping through the pages. "I'm a little rusty, but I did learn shorthand, in high school. I've a friend in the city who'd be able to help decipher it. I could help you if you stayed here, or Beryl can help you if you stay in the city. I'll contact her if you want me to."

I still found it difficult to fully trust Eve, someone I'd known for nearly a year. I'd never be able to trust someone new. On the other hand, if I stayed, allowing Eve to help me, I'd be putting her, Archie and anyone near me, in danger. Not normally superstitious, I wished for a tarot card, or some kind of message, telling me what to do.

Come on Scarlett, I told myself, as I looked at myself in the mirror in the library bathroom. *You don't need cards or psychics, follow your own intuition.* My intuition told me to leave town, temporarily, until I could figure out exactly what was happening, and why.

"What does Archie think about your plans?" Eve asked when I returned to the front desk. "I know you're close."

I gulped down the lump of anxiety that rose in my chest. "I haven't talked to Archie about this yet." I admitted. I wasn't looking forward to that conversation.

"What happens if you don't find the answers you're looking for, in the city? You might come back without finding your son, or with unresolved issues." Eve put her hand to her mouth. "I'm sorry, it's not my place to say that. Take as long as need, your job will be here when you return. Please just be careful, consider all the options. I'll help if I can."

"Thank you," I whispered, overwhelmed by her support.

"You should talk to Archie," Eve said firmly. "When you return, we can nut out the details."

ARCHIE STARED INTO his caramel thick shake. His cheese toastie was untouched on his plate. "Is there anything I can do to talk you out of leaving?"

I cringed at the level of pain I heard in my best friend's voice. "It's not forever. I'm scared that if I stay, something bad will happen to you, or Eve. You're the only two people I love, and trust and I don't want you hurt because you support me."

Archie placed his hand on top of mine. "I know you're only trying to protect the people you care about. I admire and respect that." He pushed his plate of food away, towards the middle of the table. "I've got to tell you Scarlett, I know you don't want to hear this, but I love you, and the thought of you going to the city alone, with someone trying to hurt you...I just don't know what I'd do if something happened to you."

It felt like a thousand butterflies were dancing in my stomach. I didn't want a day to pass without spending at least an hour with Archie. But with bad things were happening around me, I didn't want him in danger. "You know I don't like talking about this, but if we're being honest, I love you too, and I hate the thought of being away from you. I'd never be able to forgive myself if something bad happened to you." I didn't bother to wipe away the tears that flowed down my face. "I want to thank you, for all the things you do for me every single day," I whispered, extending my palms out to indicate the food and drink in front of us.

"Let's have dinner tonight, a date, my treat," my voice wobbled as I tried to grin. "We could have takeaway Chinese." *Our last meal together for a while,* the unspoken words on both our minds. "It's not like Forest Vale is thousands of kilometres away." I tried to lighten the mood. "I'll ring you every day, and we can message all the time." I picked up a triangle of the toastie my friend had prepared for me. "This is delicious. I'll have to come home soon; I can't cook like you." I tried for levity.

"This is true," he admitted. "You never did master the art of making a toasted cheese sandwich. I hope you don't get fat, eating all the greasy takeaways and junk food," he chuckled.

"Hah!" I snorted. "I'm not going to become some seedy private investigator, living in a dive and surviving on rubbish food." The image in my head, I could totally picture it. It could so easily become my existence. Except I had Archie and Eve.

Archie watched me as I sipped the delicious iced coffee, made with real coffee, not the sickly-sweet syrup. "Serious question," his tone one of quiet resignation. "What are you hoping to achieve by moving away? Apart from keeping me and Eve safe."

I thought about the question. "I need to decipher the shorthand notebook and understand the information Margo left for me. She must've had a reason for leaving it. I hope to find a location for Leo, I'll talk to you before I do anything silly," I promised.

"There's more." Archie wasn't asking, he knew me well enough to know when I was holding something back.

"I'm hoping I can work out if Brandon has a weak spot. To confirm why he hates me so much. It can't just be about our parents, can it? If he is behind the explosion, and my parents' death, he needs to be held accountable."

THE REST OF THE DAY flew by. Eve and I talked about her expectations and my workload while I was in the city. The most interesting visitor was Mabel. She hobbled in on her walking stick. "I hope you don't mind dear," the lady reached into her handbag and extracted a handful of flyers. She placed them on the counter. "My cousins have a bed and breakfast in the city. It's such a quaint little space for anyone who wants a holiday. Can I leave a few here, for patrons who want some time away, or maybe for writer's wanting somewhere quiet. A writer's retreat."

Eve smiled at Mabel. "We have a space for flyers on our community wall. Thank you. I'm sure some of our readers and writers would love a city break."

I googled the bed and breakfast. Located in one of the suburbs outside the city centre, with regular buses to and from the city centre. On impulse I sent an email enquiry.

Less than half an hour later I received confirmation the room was available for the next seven days. After paying in full for the accommodation, I booked a coach trip into the city. "If I don't book it now, I'm likely to chicken out and stay in West Haven," I admitted to Eve.

After a teary goodbye, I promised to check in every couple of days. "Thank you so much for having faith in me." My fingers ran along the countertop as I gathered my things. This wasn't farewell forever. I vowed to return once I knew my friends weren't in danger.

On my way to the café, I paid attention to my surroundings. Normally I walked with my head down, not making eye contact with anyone. The toy shop, the clothing store, the pharmacy, the hardware store, all part of my life in West Haven. The cars, the people running their errands, life carried on as normal. My life had changed, but around me, nothing was different. When I return after this is all over, West Haven would be the same.

"I'm glad to see you didn't run away before saying goodbye," Archie said with a grin.

"I'm not missing the opportunity for that date," I replied. "I'll order the Chinese takeaway for around six. Did you want anything else? I can stop by the supermarket."

"Dessert?" He looked up hopefully. "I'll be done cleaning in half an hour. Be careful," he added, as he collected the last of the used plates and mugs.

"WE'LL HAVE TO DO THAT again, when you return," Archie said as he collected up the empty boxes that had contained our dinner.

"Definitely," I replied.

A comfortable silence settled over us. "Do you want me to stay?" Archie asked.

I wanted to say yes. "I'll be fine. We both have an early start in the morning. I'll text you when I arrive."

Archie side-eyed me. "We'll talk on the phone every day." He emphasised the word talk, instead of texting.

"Yes, we will talk everyday," I confirmed.

We embraced at the door, neither one of us willing to let go first. Archie would have stayed. I wanted to let him.

Once he left, it felt wrong. I made a coffee and sat at my laptop. The coach departed at 6am. I set my alarm for five. Eventually I went to bed and dozed.

The noises I heard in the car park kept me in that half alert state. I couldn't be sure the noises weren't part of my nightmares as I dropped in and out of sleep. I knew it was the right decision, to keep the danger away from Archie and Eve.

Chapter Twelve

Eliza and Cora, the sisters who owned the bed and breakfast in Forest Vale were a little unusual. Their home was tucked away on a side street. I paid the taxi driver and appraised the cute, single storey, brick home. The granny flat was at the rear, past the garden, according to the internet. I guessed the building was around fifty years old, judging by the colour of the bricks and well-established gardens.

"We don't offer lunch or dinner, it's strictly a breakfast only accommodation," the taller of the two told me as they showed me to my room. The granny flat included a separate bathroom and kitchenette which contained a small fridge and a microwave. I'd noticed a small suburban shopping complex, a few blocks away where I'd be able to purchase any other food I needed.

Sisters Cora and Eliza smiled expectantly at me. Eliza, the taller of the two, wore her long black hair up in a severe ponytail. Cora was smaller, with short curly reddish blonde hair. Both wore gaudy colourful clothes and bright costume jewellery. I guessed they were in their mid-sixties. "We're so pleased you're here," said Cora, taking my hand in hers. I tried my best not to flinch at the contact of a stranger.

Eliza handed me a key. She spoke formally, like she was addressing a student. "Here's the key to the room, Scarlett. Come and go as you like. Are you here for work, or a holiday? If you don't mind me asking."

I expected questions and had prepared a story. "A little bit of both. I'm here on a research grant. I'm a writer, planning a biography of one of the well-known families of a little country town about an hour from here."

"We've heard of West Haven. You filled in your address on the application for the room," Eliza commented as she saw the puzzled look on my face. "We used to attend boarding school with some girls from there. I remember one girl, Margo was her first name. I can't remember her surname, or the names of the other girls. It was a long time ago."

Cora smiled enthusiastically. "Boarding school was such fun! I bet you know lots of lovely people, living in West Haven."

The sisters seemed friendly. I debated telling them more about me. Instead, I stuck to my promise to keep to myself. Brandon conned me so thoroughly, it'd be years before I felt I could trust people. "If you don't mind, although it wasn't a long trip, I don't travel well, and it's been a big week. I might need a nap." I yawned, as if to amplify my tiredness. In truth I was far too wired to sleep. "Or maybe I'll go for a walk, to stretch my legs, and get to know the neighbourhood."

"What a good idea," Cora smiled. "You'll settle in, in no time. Just remember to protect yourself and let us know what you want for breakfast by 5pm the day before. The breakfast forms are on the table in your room, with the Wi-Fi password."

I must've looked puzzled. I had no idea what Cora meant by *protect yourself*.

"Goodness gracious, don't tell me you don't know about protecting yourself! You do know you're an empath, don't you?" Eliza commented, looking at me with wide saucer eyes.

My stomach turned somersaults. I didn't like the way the conversation had turned towards me. "Um, I've heard of empathy, and empath – is it a real word, or some new age term to help explain anxiety?" Why was I talking about this with two strangers?

The sisters saw my discomfort. Cora patted her sister's arm. "Let's leave her to settle in. Scarlett doesn't need to know about all that now. We can chat over breakfast one day."

Eliza looked over the top of her glasses, assessing me. I wanted to hide from her discerning eyes, but I wasn't sure why. "Hmm, okay. Enjoy the rest of the day. Knock on the door if you need anything. Otherwise, we'll see you tomorrow morning at breakfast." The sisters turned and left the room. I breathed a sigh of relief. I shook off the scrutiny of the sisters, as curiosity.

The smell of the cars, trucks and buses zipping past me made me wrinkle my nose. I didn't like noises, smells, lights, or crowds. Living in the city would be horrible if I didn't conquer my sensory sensitivities. University had been an exciting adventure. This trip was made of necessity. I exhaled, trying to rid my mouth of the taste of exhaust fumes.

The footpath across the suburb took me through a corner park, past rows of houses and townhouses. The residences were of a similar style. I walked past a school, and some older houses. Old brick homes with garages, carports and neat gardens. The shopping complex of the same dreary brick sat a few blocks over from the sisters. An easy twenty-minute walk.

The stroll helped clear my head. "You'd like Eliza and Cora," I told Archie, keeping my promise to let him know as soon as I arrived. "They're cute little old ladies, straight out of a witchy book, or cozy murder mystery." I found myself smiling as I described my temporary land ladies.

"I hope they don't cook for you, otherwise you'll decide to stay there," Archie joked, but I heard the sadness in his voice.

"No one can cook as well as you," I promised. "Speaking of, I have a microwave in my room, so I can make mac and cheese." I tried to sound like I was on a holiday, and not hiding from an intimidating bully. "The local shop has a decent mini supermarket, and a café. Nothing like yours of course, but it's a place to sit and work out my next move."

DAY ONE MY ALARM WOKE me up at 6am. The sisters arranged breakfast at 8am, which gave me a couple of hours for a walk. I walked further than the day before, and in the opposite direction. I planned a reconnoitre so I knew of all possible ways of entering and leaving the area, and any other retail complexes within walking distance.

"I guess most people who live around here, travel into the city. I couldn't find any other options for cafes, or shops." I told Archie he rang to check on me. "It's just rows and rows of houses, townhouses, childcare centres, and a school or two. If I lived here, I'd stay inside, or move, it's too depressing. After breakfast with the sisters, I'll check out the café and do some research. It looked like the centre had complimentary internet access."

The conversation ended with me promising to be careful. I wiped away a stray tear, as I took a short cut through a park. The trees were large, old, and provided shade for the amenities in the green space. Faded wooden park bench seats, wooden tables, and a couple of tired old barbeques betrayed the age of the suburb. Even the play equipment needed updating. The swings held my weight, but I wouldn't want to fall on the tan bark underneath it. The metal slippery dip would be a challenge during summer.

I'll only take you to the newer playgrounds, with rubbery soft fall underneath brightly coloured, thick plastic equipment. I whispered to Leo.

The dwellings closer to the sisters were bigger, as if I were now in the more affluent section of suburbia. An involuntary shiver ran down my spine. My idea to run away to the city wasn't nearly as appealing in reality. This suburb was drab, with no personality or warmth. A place to live when not at work or school, even the front gardens felt sterile. The obligatory hedge bushes, tall thin trees, small non flowery shrubs, looked bored and abandoned.

The sister's garden was different. As I walked through the front gate of the bed and breakfast, a beautiful display of roses greeted me. Most of the bushes were in flower. Red, pink and yellow blossoms greeted me. Opening the wooden side gate into the generous outdoor area I found myself under a huge wisteria twined with jasmine and a third vine that covered the roof of the wooden pergola. To my left and right were an assortment of flowering plants and bushes, with a couple of taller trees providing shade.

I took out my key, and was about to enter my room, when I heard a noise behind me. "Good morning, Scarlett!" I turned to see Cora standing beside their wooden outdoor setting, which was decked out with juice, coffee, toast and fruit, exactly as I'd ordered it from the list of available breakfast foods. "I hope this is to your liking."

The taller sister added a tray of muffins to the table. "You can choose different foods each day if you like, we have a well-stocked larder." Eliza indicated with her hand that I should sit in the empty seat closest to me.

"What are you up to today?" Cora asked. "I see you've returned home from a walk already. We like to wake up early and get all our chores done before the day starts."

I sipped the delicious fresh squeezed orange juice. "I'm keen to get stuck into my research. From my couple of walks it looks like the best option is the café in the shopping complex. Coffee and free internet to get some initial work underway. I can hop on a bus when I need to check out the library." I chose orange marmalade for my toast. A condiment I'd not eaten for years, it reminded me of Christmas morning, when my mother would open all the little jars of breakfast spread in the hampers we'd been gifted by Dad's patients. I've a few pages of shorthand I'll need deciphering soon, I'm sure I'll find someone in the city who can do that."

"Make sure to be careful if you're on the bus, or in a crowd, you won't be used to it," Cora spoke so quietly I had to lean in to catch her words. When I did, I wasn't entirely sure what she meant.

I was about to ask her, when her sister addressed me. "I can't wait to read your book, once it's published." Eliza's eyes drilled into mine, over her cup of tea.

"Hopefully my work will live up to expectations." I met her stare, unsure why I felt nauseous. Maybe because she reminded me of the stern headmistress at my primary school. It was an odd coincidence that they went to school with Margo all those years ago. Mum had mentioned that a lot of the richer families sent their children away to boarding school. I dismissed my uneasiness as anxiety, or paranoia. The sisters weren't working for Brandon.

"I can't remember what you said, my brains like a sieve these days," Cora's voice broke into my thoughts. "Did you say you were being funded or are you living off your savings? It can get expensive here in the city."

Did I give that much detail away the day before? I didn't think so. I took her question as harmless interest. "I have a generous employer," was all I chose to say, before taking a bite of an orange poppyseed muffin.

"Do take some food with you, or to keep in your room, if you're finished breakfast," Eliza said as I wiped my mouth with the red napkin provided.

I surveyed the food remaining on the table, wondering what they did with the leftovers. "Breakfast was lovely, thank you. I might take an apple and a banana, for later." Staying at the bed and breakfast ate into my savings a little, but the breakfast was only ten dollars extra a day, which seemed good value for money.

AFTER CLEANING UP, and packing my laptop into my handbag, I walked the few blocks to the shopping complex I'd discovered the day before. What did Cora mean, about being careful in a crowd or a bus. Was she referring to me specifically, or a general comment about personal safety? Maybe it related to the conversation the day before, about empaths and empathy. Did other people have trouble reading people and understanding conversations?

I'd been called nervous, anxious, highly strung, and the word empath may have been used before, but I tended to block out comments about my mental health. My anxiety caused me enough trouble, without getting stressed about other people's opinions of me. That two virtual strangers mentioned the word empath as related to me, maybe I should consider reading up on it.

After I sorted my current dilemma. I shook my head to clear all thoughts of my own state of health. The way the sisters acted, I half expected them to have a crystal ball, tarot cards, or offer a seance to find my answers for my research.

I watched a group of teens waiting for the bus. Three were kicking a ball, another three crouched over their mobiles. I'd hate to be in their shoes. Societies expectations, peer pressure, parental and teacher rules could be overwhelming. Diagnoses of anxiety and depression carried less stigma than ten years ago. People were less afraid to name their conditions, and more willing to embrace alternate ways of dealing with fears and phobias. I'd felt restless and out of place my whole life. From a home where my parents were aloof and busy, to a university that didn't offer me the degree I wanted... *Focus, Scarlett.* I muttered as I got closer to the shopping centre. *You're not that awkward teenager anymore.*

The barista didn't remind me of Archie in the slightest. Bertha was large, with a hearty laugh, and friendly smile, and bright purple hair. "You can sit right there for as long as you like. Just order some food, or coffee occasionally. Here's the Wi-Fi password." She passed me a business card with a code on one side.

"Thanks. I'll have a large mocha, to start with, and a bottle of water. Also, a piece of that yummy looking chocolate cake please."

"Coming right up!" Bertha smiled as she turned to the coffee machine. I chose a booth in one corner, facing the front door. I felt more comfortable able to see people coming and going. With my back against the wall, and I could also see the back door. I laughed at how jumpy I was. If Brandon was trying to scare me, I doubt he'd find me tucked away here in suburbia.

After the first half hour, where every time the door opened, I glanced up to see who was ordering, I settled down to work. The deal Eve and I agreed on included me planning every detail of the Book Week activities and calling in once a week to discuss. We planned a weekly zoom meeting for Thursdays, so I had a few days to prepare. With pages of notes on the week-long festival celebrating books and authors, I planned on doing library work in the evenings.

My biggest problem was the notebook full of shorthand, and I had no idea what the scribbles meant. "I don't suppose you know anyone locally who can read shorthand?" I asked Bertha as she arrived at my table with a tray laden with goodies.

"I don't know anyone personally," she said as she unloaded my mug, water bottle, and cake. "Check out the noticeboard on the wall," she indicated the wall near the front door. "People pop up all sorts of things. You could always post up a note, asking for anyone who could read shorthand to contact you."

"That's not a bad idea," I mused. "Thanks."

I set up a fake social media account under the name Abigail Flowers. No pictures, just a woman who loved to garden, reading historical romances and who worked at a publishing company in the city. I kept the blurb simple, that I was researching for a local history book I was commissioned to write. I joined a couple of groups I thought may have information, I wasn't keen to start out by asking for anyone who could read shorthand. I wasn't sure how far Brandon's reach was on social media.

"Not a bad first day," I told Archie as I walked back to my accommodation. "Bertha's coffee and cakes aren't as good as yours. I set up a fake social media account, and I've written an action plan. I also put in a couple of hours work for my real job. I'm looking forward to Book Week."

"So am I, if it means you'll be home by then," Archie quipped. I could tell he was still upset with me leaving.

"That's my plan. Turns out I don't like the city at all. It's a means to an end, that's all." My heart felt lighter after talking to Archie. I knew he felt the same.

Armed with a microwave macaroni and cheese from the supermarket, with a gooey chocolate dessert I waved at the sisters as I headed to my room. I didn't feel like engaging with them about my day. Whether or not the term empath meant anything, I felt exhausted, not just from the walking. I changed into my pyjamas and curled up on the bed while my dinner twirled around in the microwave.

At the ding of the cooking appliance, I reluctantly uncurled myself and moved to the table. With a bottle of water, my dinner and laptop, and the television on in the background for company I was set for the night. The mac and cheese tasted surprisingly good for a TV dinner. I polished off the dessert with an instant coffee. Grateful the sisters suggested I bring the leftover fruit to my room, I nibbled the banana while I read through some information on the Watsons, that I'd managed to find online. When I heard a beep signifying an email, I wasn't surprised to see the message *Stop, or you'll be sorry* pop up on my screen. I pressed delete, without reading any further. Ignoring the pounding of my heart, I closed my laptop and concentrated on the comedy show on television.

Chapter Thirteen

Day two didn't start according to plan. I slept in later than I'd hoped. I'd spent most of the night tossing and turning as faceless men in black chased me waving pages of a notebook. I debated going for a walk, but my legs ached from the number of steps over the last day or so. I settled for stretches and sit ups while I waited for breakfast.

"We've been thinking about your project, and we think we can help," Cora passed the jug of juice towards me as I joined them at the table.

I chose a selection of fresh fruits and a banana muffin. "It's nice of you to offer." I decided there was no harm in hearing them out. "What do you have in mind?"

Eliza finished her mouthful of warm banana muffin. "Don't laugh, but we belong to a puzzle club. Each week we meet and solve a cryptic puzzle. It could be based on a board game, a jigsaw puzzle, a detective book. Anyway, we met yesterday, and we think it'll be fun to solve the puzzle of your shorthand notebook."

"There's this too," Cora handed me a small book entitled *I'm not crazy, I'm an empath*. The last bite of muffin sat heavy in my stomach. Sharing information with strangers suddenly felt too real. Vulnerable. My inability to trust manifested in pains in my stomach.

My appetite had vanished, by my manners hadn't. I couldn't leave the fruit uneaten on my plate. I slowly nibbled on the strawberries and pieces of banana, as I looked at the pale blue cover of the book and flicked through the pages. Slowly placing the book on the table. I sipped my mocha, letting the bittersweet mix of chocolate and caffeine clear my mind. What was I scared of? Eve and Archie were safely out of harm's way and Brandon had no idea where I was. These two sweet little ladies were in no danger. I didn't have to be their best friend. I could thank them for the book and trust them enough to hand Margo's book over for deciphering. Even if they were at school with Margo briefly, sixty years ago, they weren't connected to West Haven.

Both women stared at me, waiting for me to respond. I looked around at the well cared for garden. Whether or not I trusted the women, I was here to find answers. "Thank you, for lending me the book, I'll read and return it while I'm here. Please also thank your group for me. I'll photocopy the notebook today. When does your group meet again?" I tried to ignore the thumping of my heart. I came here for answers, it would do no good to ignore or avoid opportunities to find them.

"The newsagent at the shopping centre up the road has a copier. Tell them it's for our group and you'll get a discount. There's five of us in the group. Three copies should do us though," Cora said helpfully.

"We're meeting this afternoon at 2pm as it happens," Eliza added. "We were excited at the idea of deciphering the shorthand."

Back in my room I counted the pages of the notebook. Five double pages of neatly scribbled hieroglyphics times three, wouldn't be too costly. I hadn't asked the sisters when the group thought they'd solve the puzzle, but they sounded keen. Fingers crossed that meant a resolution sooner than I'd originally anticipated.

"How's the café going?" I asked Archie, after telling him of the latest developments.

"Cafés busy. Pippa's learning barista skills, which is great. The customers love her unique blend of coffee with vanilla syrup. She wants to add more unusual flavours like lavender, gingerbread, pumpkin spice." I could hear the pride in Archie's voice, and the eye rolling. "I've added new flavours to the chocolate brownies, to compliment her idea. I wish you were here to taste test for me. The book club ladies seem to love them."

This time it was my turn to roll my eyes. "The book club ladies love you, Archie. They'd devour you if they could. Not jealous over here, but I want you in one piece when I return home."

If I didn't overthink it, a temporary trip to the city wasn't so bad. I talked to Archie at least twice a day and breakfast was made for me. I enjoyed the walk to and from the café, once I got used to the sensory overload, and I still got paid for working with Eve.

The newsagent was located next to the café, a route I knew reasonably well by now. I detoured across the park. Children passed me on their way to school. The noise of the traffic wasn't too bad, the main road into the city located one block to my right. I noticed a bus stop, mainly because there were a few people congregated. I quickly skimmed the timetable. Not that I planned a trip into the city but if I did need to, buses stopped here every half an hour during business hours.

Errol, the owner of the newsagents stood a good head taller than me, and broad. At least ten years older than me, and bald. His reading glasses sat high on top of his shiny head. "You must be Cora's lodger," he said amiably. "If this is for Cora's group, I can do five copies, six if you want one yourself, for only ten dollars."

"Sounds terrific, thanks Errol. Do you mind if I browse while I wait?" I didn't want to hurry him up, but I wasn't keen to let the book out of my sight.

"Go right ahead. This won't take me long." Errol flipped a switch and the multi-function copier sprung to life with a hum.

By the time Errol returned to the counter with the notebook and copies I'd chosen myself a notebook, a pack of coloured pens, and a couple of murder mysteries to pass the time. I briefly considered a couple of gardening magazines until I remembered with a lump in my throat that I no longer had a garden.

Bertha waved at me as I passed the café. I waved back and smiled at the barista as she wiped down the empty table out the front of her shop. I contemplated a mocha, but I wanted to get the photocopies back to Eliza and Cora as soon as possible. As I walked outside the complex, prepared to walk back, a taxi pulled up. An elderly man with a walking stick climbed out of the vehicle. I took advantage of the empty cab and a grabbed a lift back.

I declined the sisters' invitation to join their puzzle group. I'd be a nervous wreck if I had to sit through someone deciphering Margo's scribbles. Rather than getting the message in dribs and drabs, I'd prefer the whole story in one chunk. Not that I worded it that way to the ladies. "I do appreciate that the puzzle group wants to help me decipher the code," I smiled at them. "I've got some work I want to finish today, for a Thursday deadline." It wasn't a lie.

Once I'd delivered the pages, I'd planned to settle into some work for Eve. Instead, I found myself walking past the bus stop, as a bus pulled in on its way into the city. I rummaged in my bag for my travel card as I joined the two goth looking youth and three older ladies waiting to board. We zoomed by houses, densely populated townhouses, and tall apartment complexes. As we merged onto a main road, and crept closer to the city, all the worn, tired shopfronts looked the same. Fast food from around the world, tobacconists, wine cellars, tattoo parlours, and twenty-four-hour convenience stores.

Soon the scenery took on a more opulent feel. The shoddy housing replaced by wealthy high rises and posh shopping complexes. The familiar rise of panic rose in my stomach as we got closer to the crowds. Even before the bus stopped at the terminal my hands were clammy.

You can do this. I told myself, my fingers nervously tapping on my handbag. My arms protectively crossed across my bag, even though no one sat anywhere near me. It contained my laptop, the notebook and all my important items. I kept it in front of me as I exited the bus.

The noises, smells, and number of people made me nauseous. I walked along the path, head down, imagining I was in a bubble protecting me from harm. Any notion of living in the city evaporated in the harsh light of reality, amongst the crowd that surged forward on their way to whatever destination called them.

The aroma of freshly made coffee nearly drew me into the coffee shop named *Do Drop Inn*. As someone exited with three coffees and muffins balanced on a tray, I noticed the line to the counter and kept walking. The next three coffee shops were as busy. Patrons with their eyes focused on their phones as they waited to order, or for their order to be filled. A sign and a large glass front entrance indicated a one of those shopping complexes with over fifty speciality shops. Rather than turning and running in the other direction I headed through the doors towards the bright lights. Today the glitter and sparkle felt safer than the darker, cosy corner coffee shops. A crowd of shoppers preferable to the determined mass of people on the footpath.

I chose a booth in the open near a donut shop that offered two cinnamon treats with a large cappuccino. I took my laptop out of my bag, pleased the centre offered free Wi-Fi for its patrons. My taste buds didn't like the initial shock of the bitter brew without the sweetness of cocoa to soften it. Still, I managed to finish it and a second coffee. I balanced the bitterness by polishing off two cinnamon donuts and a chocolate covered one as well.

My foot tapped nervously. The soft black sole of my boots making no sound on the shiny floor. My eyes kept wandering to the digital clock on the wall above the information booth in the middle of the atrium. Waiting for the secrets of the notebook to be revealed was excruciating. With the internet to distract me I looked up Brandon's name, and Gerald Watson. While there were no pictures, by trying the combination of their names together I found a Watson and Kelly

Attorneys at Law. I choked on my mouthful of coffee as I noted their office address wasn't on the far side of the country, but not far from the shopping centre where I was located. I closed the search browser and slammed shut my laptop, looking around furtively as if Brandon or Gerald were lurking ready to pounce.

Maybe two strong cappuccinos in a row wasn't such a good idea after all. I grinned, hearing Archie's voice in my head, about how I should stick to mocha and not go full on Scarlett mode. His term for when I used to live off coffee and chocolate. While he fed my sweet tooth, he made sure I balanced it with other foods. "May I have a banana smoothie please?" I asked the young lady with long blonde hair and mascara, disinterested in the job that paid her wages.

"Have whatever you'd like," she surprised me by responding with a more than one words answer. "The coffee would be making you jittery. At least it does for my nan."

I couldn't hide my smile as I tried to work out whether to be offended. I was no more than ten years older than the blonde star child in front of me. Her nan indeed. "I've a way to go before I'm anyone's nan," I said conversationally. I decided to take the smoothie 'to go,' and wandered past several shop windows as I slurped my drink through the paper straw. The multiple dress shops reminded me of my limited wardrobe. I glanced at my faded jeans and supermarket t-shirt. Discarding my drink once the straw became too soggy to be functional, my feet led me into the department store. On the hunt for distractions to fill the gap until it was time to head back.

The purple suitcase attracted my attention first. Then the purple shoes, another pair of blue jeans, and three tops of the price of two. Before I knew it, I had chosen new underwear and replenished my toiletries as well. The alarm I'd set on my watch told me the puzzle group would have just sat down to meet. "Can I help with anything?" A woman I estimated to be in her forties smiled from where she was filling up the lollies and chocolates.

"What do you recommend? For a friend who's helping me with a project?" My mind was still thinking about the puzzle club, wondering when it would be reasonable to expect an answer.

The woman leant to her right. "How about a box of chocolates? I find they make a great thank you gift for all ages." I thanked the lady and pondered the assortment of sweet treats in front of me. I chose a large flat box that'd fit in the purple travel bag with my other purchases. I wandered the store for a while longer, eventually making my way to the checkout.

Pulling, or pushing, the travel bag proved easier than I thought. Much easier than lugging multiple shopping bags around. I walked through the centre on the way to the bus stop. I dawdled, until the clock above the jewellers clicked over to 3pm. The butterflies in my stomach jostled among the partially digested sugary treats. Had the women already deciphered any of the notebook? How long would it take? I was driving myself crazy. Archie and Eve were always so calm and patient, I needed to figure out how they managed it. I'd missed the life lesson on how to stay in control of raging emotions. *Be reasonable Scarlett.* Day two, or three, if I counted my traveling day. The progress wasn't too bad, all things considered.

The news that Gerald and Brandon possibly worked and lived not far from where I stood, did nothing to help settle my stomach. I'd wait and continue that search when I felt calmer, and further away from their office space. I kept my head down, imagining Brandon lucking at every corner, I wished I'd worn a hoodie. In the absence of an item of clothing to wrap around myself, I sat huddled in the corner of the bus shelter. The next bus to the sisters' suburb wasn't due for twenty minutes.

Chapter Fourteen

Cora clapped her hands together as I walked through the garden on my way to my room. "Oh, goodie, you're back." With her enthusiasm and her frilly layered skirt and blouse, she reminded me of an happy little girl. "Why don't you put your things away and come in for tea."

Eliza eyed my new purple bag. "It looks like you've been on a shopping spree," she commented.

"Honestly, the bag was on special and it's an easier option for traveling on a bus than multiple shopping bags. I don't think I told you, but there was a freak accident where I lived, and I lost everything." Why did I tell them that? I hadn't planned on sharing any personal information. I immediately regretted my overshare. "I'd love a cuppa, I'll just put this in my room." I trundled the suitcase quickly, not giving the ladies a chance to ask questions.

When I opened the glass sliding door, Cora and Eliza were already seated at their kitchen table. A large round piece of furniture it took up most of the space between their external door and the kitchen benches. The wood had age to it, scuffs and scratches told me the item had hosted many special occasions. The chairs around the table, made of the same deep red wood, had thick material cushioned seats. On the table sat a large metal teapot in a black cozy, and three thick blue mugs. A matching blue milk jug and sugar bowl sat beside the tea pot. A plate of lamingtons sat near a bowl of strawberries.

The room was darker than it looked from the outside, on account of the thick blue curtains covering the windows and sliding door, and the dark green painted walls. Weirdly, none of it looked gaudy. I felt like I'd stepped into a room in an old castle or stately home. Thankfully my room was light, white and fresh, I'd have been claustrophobic in such a dark living space.

Eliza held the teapot just above my mug. "Tea?" she asked, pouring it before I managed to answer her.

"Do have some lamingtons and strawberries," Cora added, popping a couple of both on my plate.

I only briefly wondered if they were safe to eat and drink. Brandon, or whoever was behind weird things happening to and around me, couldn't have steered me towards two little old ladies who'd slowly poison me with food, tea, and kindness, could he? I laughed at myself, internally, so I didn't appear crazy. "Thank you, this all looks yummy. Thank you for the tea, it's just what I needed."

"We love having someone to spoil, and well, we don't want to pry, but we'd love to know more of your story, if you wish to share it," Cora said gently.

"It turns out we know more than you realise, thanks to Betty," Eliza set the teapot down.

I must've looked puzzled, because Cora added quickly, "Betty knows shorthand. She had your notebook deciphered before we finished our sandwiches."

"Oh," I wasn't sure what else to say except, "Thank you, to you both and to Betty and your puzzle group." I'd not considered the personal information they may glean about me, being able to read shorthand.

"Why don't you take the papers, and read it, after we finish tea. Then you can decide if you want to tell us any more of your story. You totally don't have to, but we would love to help, if we could," Cora said.

My feet fidgeted under the table, as Eliza poured me a second cup of tea. Cora added more cakes and berries to my plate. "Where did you find that lovely purple bag?" she asked conversationally.

"In a department store at the shopping centre in town." All I wanted was to grab the notebook pages and the puzzle group's deciphering of it and head straight to my room. The sisters wanted to chat. Didn't they get enough conversation at their group?

"We go on an outing every week, but not on the bus," Eliza wrinkled her nose. "Our charming nephew pays for a taxi to take us to wherever we want to go. Not just any taxi, it's a silver service car."

"He pays for a posh lunch as well." Cora's enthusiasm returned.

"Your nephew sounds thoughtful, to take such good care of you both," I smiled, noting an absence of photographs in the room. The shelves behind us held hundreds of books, half a dozen used candles and a collection of miniature tea pots. "Does he visit, or join you for lunch?"

"Oh, my goodness no, Elton lives overseas, he runs the family business." Cora stopped abruptly. I felt movement under the table. Did Eliza just kick her sister? I decided not to ask any other questions.

Eliza glared at her over the rim of her glasses, nodding at me. "We should let Scarlett go to her room. She probably wants to read the long hand version of the notebook." The older sister's tone left no room for debate.

Thanking the sisters for their hospitality I clutched the notebook and the neatly written deciphered pages and headed back to my room. My heart pounded so heavily in my chest I wondered if I was about to suffer a heart attack. Could I be about to discover where Brandon was keeping Leo?

I closed and locked the door out of habit, though I didn't think anyone would be attacking me here in the bottom of the garden. After pouring myself a glass of water, and splashing cold water on my face, I sat at the table.

Scarlett, apologies for not helping you while I was alive. When you first returned and your parents refused to help, I wanted to reach out. I couldn't. Families can be complicated. You've read the newspaper clippings. That's only the tip of the problems between the Nightlys and the Kellys. The Watsons are related to both families through marriages. None of us are what we seem, we all try so hard to hide the past, we forget about the present and the future.

My brother adopted Brandon as a small boy, and though they only lived in West Haven briefly I could see he was troubled. His parents died under suspicious circumstances. Their bitterness about people who wronged them gave birth to the monster he became. Gerald tried to make Brandon see there were other ways of living, rather than revenge, anger, and deception. When that didn't work, he supported Brandon as Leo's caregiver, hoping that having a child to raise would change Brandon for the better.

Leo is a beautiful little boy, full of love, life, and laughter. Brandon has found him a full-time nanny who is teaching him right from wrong. They all live at Gerald's property, in Forest Vale. 123 Oak Drive. Don't try to access the property to rescue Leo, it's heavily fortified with security guards and an electric fence. Gerald and Brandon own an attorney firm in Forest Vale. Together they are a formidable pair.

Brandon has created a fortress around himself and his son. I don't think you will be able to save him if that's what you're planning after reading this. I suggest you contact Nanny Alma via the Oak Drive address. She might send you photos and update you about your son's progress through life. He will receive everything money can buy. You could talk to Nanny Alma about sending birthday cards and the like, and maybe one day you may be able to visit...

Margo's words stopped there. No matter how many times I flipped the pages over, I didn't find any additional words from beyond the grave. *What was the point of telling me where you are dear child, to then tell me not to visit?*

How long I sat in silence staring at the written words on the page I wasn't sure, the beeping of my mobile broke me from my trance. I stared at the caller ID – Archie. I knew I should answer, I wanted to, but I couldn't move. Whether it was anger, sadness, anxiety, frustration, I couldn't name exactly how I felt.

"It's like I'm three steps closer, but also so far away." I tried to explain to Archie a few minutes later when I dragged myself together and returned his call.

"Come home so I can look after you, or I could close the café and come to you." I heard the angst in his voice, being so far away and not able to help.

"I'll be home soon. I promise. I need to..." my voice trailed off as I wasn't exactly sure what I needed to do. Somehow, I had to make sure that not only was Leo safe, but Archie and Eve as well.

"I know, I understand, I just don't like it." Archie sounded so close. "Just remember to eat something healthy every day, not just coffee and chocolate." My best mate knew me so well. "I'll ring you early in the morning."

I re-read the message from beyond the grave. Something didn't feel right. I couldn't put my finger on what. Why give me the address, tell me it was heavily guarded, and advise me against trying to visit? Why would the nanny, employed by Brandon, be teaching my son right from wrong, when he didn't appear to live any semblance of those values in his own life? Was it Gerald's influence?

Google maps wasn't much help. According to the computer screen 123 Oak Drive didn't exist. Forest Vale didn't have an Oak Drive at all. The nearest Oak Drive was in another town, the highest block number being fifty. Could the puzzle group have mis-read or mis-interpreted the shorthand?

I knew my brain was muddled. I needed to clear it. Maybe a walk would help. After the fire and everything that happened, I couldn't leave my laptop behind, not even here, where no one knew me. I piled all the information from Margo into my handbag as well, slinging the strap over my shoulder. Cora and Eliza waved as I passed the sliding door.

It was after 4pm and a little chilly. I quickened my pace, regretting not picking up my cardigan. Choosing a new path, in a direction I'd not tried before, I soon came across an older suburban row of shops. A little pizza and pasta takeaway, a hot chips and burger café, and something I'd not seen before, an internet wine bar.

Deciding on the latter purely for the free Wi-Fi, I sighed with relief when it wasn't dingy inside. Olive green and cream décor gave the space an elegant feel. It reminded me of Archie's café, with the bar that ran along the wall in front of the kitchen. Whereas Archie's shelf contained coffee beans, and a large range of syrups, the shelf here offered a large range of wines in wine racks, with glasses hanging by their stems from the ceiling. Modern, sleek chairs and tables, a couple of higher benches with stools, and some comfy sofas ensured lots of spaces for patrons to sit and drink, eat, chat, or work.

The tall woman behind the counter wore a bright blue pants suit. Her black hair tied in a high ponytail. "Hello, my name's Marta. What can I get you today? Our afternoon special is nachos and your choice of wine," she smiled.

"The nachos sound nice," I responded, not realising how hungry I was until she mentioned food. "Is it possible to get a soda water and lime, instead of wine?"

"Of course it is. I can keep a tab open for you; in case you feel like coffee and dessert after." She motioned to the seating area. "Choose any of the tables without reserved signs. I'll bring your drink and food over to you."

"Dessert and coffee sounds like a good idea and thank you." I gravitated towards the table with the chair facing out towards the room. Comfortable with the idea no one would be behind me. I pulled out my laptop, placed my bag on the seat next to me, and opened a new search window.

Not sure what to look up, I had a weird prickling sensation warning me I was missing some important piece of information. I startled as Marta arrived at the table with my meal and tall glass of soda and lime. "I didn't mean to scare you," she said gently. "I haven't seen you in here before, are you new to the area?"

"I'm staying at a B and B not too far away, working on a project." I was distracted, trying to figure out why I felt uneasy.

"It sounds fascinating. Enjoy your meal and let me know if you decide on dessert." Marta smiled as she left, to serve the customers who'd just entered the wine bar.

The tasty cheese, avocado, chilli, and other flavours gave my taste buds a merry dance. I ate slowly, letting my mind wander over the events of the last few weeks. After losing Leo, I ended up with a trauma induced anxiety. It'd taken nearly four years, Archie's patience, and the job in the library, to pull me out, but I was almost in a place where I could function 'normally' whatever that meant. I'd always miss Leo, and want him with me, but I'd had to learn to let go.

I looked up as Marta stopped by my table. "I didn't mean to disturb you, it looked like you were deep in thought. I get you anything else?"

The plate that held my nachos was empty, and so was my glass. "The coffee and dessert you mentioned before sounds lovely." As my eyes focused on the space around me, I noticed most of the customers who'd been seated when I arrived had left. How long had I been staring into space, eating nachos?

Marta returned with a mug and a plate of mud cake with chocolate ice cream. "Today's special," she grinned. "I may be over stepping, but if you'd like to talk anything through, I can sit with you, until more customers come in."

I stared at Marta. She made me feel at ease and reminded me of Eve. After tonight, I'd never see her again. It wouldn't hurt, to tell her part of my story. "I have a hard time trusting anyone, but I'll go crazy if I don't talk this through with someone."

If I was Marta, I would have made my excuses and left. Instead, she commented, "Tell me as much or as little as you feel comfortable. You mentioned a project?"

"Yes, the project, I may have stretched the truth. Although I am working on a Book Week project for the library where I work. I'm here on personal reasons." I ended up telling Marta the whole story, starting with meeting Brandon at university and ending with the deciphering of the shorthand notebook.

She returned to my table after serving a group of businessmen their wine and nachos. "Would you like me to tell you my thoughts on your story?" she asked tentatively.

"Yes please," I felt a calm I'd not felt since before I came across Gerald Watson in the library. That encounter had started me down this rabbit warren of secrets and lies.

"It sounds to me, like someone is pulling the strings, orchestrating all the events of the last few weeks. Think back to when you were growing up, with your parents. Did they ever mention Brandon, the Kellys, or the Watsons other than in general conversation?"

I considered the question. "Everyone knew Margo and the Watsons. They were one of the towns wealthiest families. Mum and Dad would sometimes go to parties she hosted, but nothing else stands out. I was a nerdy kid, social anxiety I think it's called now. When I wasn't studying, I had my nose stuck in a book."

"What about Gerald?" Marta asked.

"I don't think I knew Margo had a brother, though I wouldn't have paid attention to that sort of thing. Until I overheard him mention Brandon in the library, I hadn't realised Margo had died. If I'm not at work or with Archie at the café, I'm at home. I don't read the papers or listen to the news."

"This might sound far-fetched," Marta continued, "But what if Brandon is somehow keeping tabs on you, noticed how well you're doing and set up recent events, to throw you back into a depression?"

Running my mind back through the last couple of weeks, I tried to figure out if Marta could be right. "So, are you suggesting that Brandon paid, or coerced, Gerald to say all that in front of me? He couldn't have killed Margo, could he? It's easy to believe he convinced a local to vandalise the books and cause the explosion. He can be persuasive." I felt the colour drain from my face as I thought of something. "You don't think he killed my parents too? And how would he make Mr Sinclair, the local solicitor to set up the meeting with me, about Margo's estate?"

Marta tilted her head to one side, checking no customers were waiting. "You said Brandon was a lawyer? Could he have somehow gotten Mr Sinclair to lie? Do you know the man you spoke to is a lawyer?" The door opened and a crowd of noisy revellers entered. "Just something to think about. Do some more research. Don't rely on what you think you know. Also, maybe delve deeper into the background of the women you're staying with." Marta stood, headed back to the counter and welcomed the newcomers.

Wishing I'd asked for another coffee, and a bottle of water, I scanned the room. No one seemed familiar, or the slightest bit interested in me. Is it paranoid to assume someone is pulling strings to make you behave and act in a certain way? Or that they are bribing others to do their handiwork? If what Marta suggested were true, it sounded more like a plot from a story, rather than real life.

Life is stranger than fiction, whispered a little voice inside my head. I picked up my phone to call Archie. I put it back down. Could my phone be bugged? Could my laptop? There was only one way to be certain. It'd cost money, luckily, I'd managed to save enough for what I had to do. I made use of the wine bars automatic teller machine and withdraw a large amount of cash.

Chapter Fifteen

Marta agreed to let me use the bar's phone to book a room in a motel on the other side of the city, and a taxi. We hugged as I hopped into the taxi. Rather than the overwhelm and anxiety I normally experienced, I felt exhilarated, in control for the first time for a long time.

I offered the friendly taxi driver extra money to wait while I gathered my things. He happily kept his car idling across the road from the bed and breakfast. I crept past the glass door; grateful the house was dark. Hopefully the sisters were asleep. It only took a couple of minutes to pack my belongings into the purple bag and returned to the taxi.

The trip across the city took twenty minutes. I'd chosen a big motel chain, one close to shops, and the bus and train stations. The taxi driver drove off, happy with his tip. He offered to drive me, if I needed to go anywhere else during my stay in the city.

Tim, at the reception desk was cheerfully and chatty. I asked if he knew of any local tech shops where I could get a new laptop and mobile but not lose all my files. He gave me the address of a shop near the shopping centre that should be able to help.

How could I let Eve and Archie knew I moved? If Marta's assumption proved correct, I didn't want to risk alerting Brandon to my new location. In my gut what she suggested made sense. Brandon would go to any length to keep me away from Leo. If he knew I was getting stronger, he'd be looking for a way to shake my confidence.

I spent a restless night in a room where I should have enjoyed the luxury of crisp white sheets, matching towels and a bathrobe. I chose to head to the dining room for an early breakfast of cereal, toast, fruit and a couple of little pastries. To fortify myself for the day ahead. I headed back to my room to clean my teeth. Before I locked the door, I hid the notebook and file under the mattress, although I now doubted the authenticity of the information. Thinking about the conversation with Marta, it made more sense that Brandon set me up. Why would a lady I didn't know, leave me a set of documents in a safety deposit box? If the bartender was correct, Brandon had gone to great lengths to keep me paranoid and anxious – both traits that would make me appear an unfit mother.

As I put my laptop and mobile into my handbag, I wondered if someone could have bugged my handbag. Was I over-reacting? Had I reached a whole new level of paranoia? I heaved a sigh as I remembered how much I liked the bag when I bought it. To be on the safe side, I'd donate it and replace it with a new one.

Finally, at 8:30am I headed back to the foyer, and checked the complimentary motel computer for directions to the tech shop that Tim recommended. I spotted a cab outside the motel. I decided to taxi to the shopping complex, thankful for the cash I'd withdrawn, making it more difficult for Brandon to find me. Unless he had a tracking device in my handbag.

"WHY ARE YOU RINGING from a new number? And why didn't you answer my call earlier?" Archie sounded frantic when I finally sat down and dialled his number.

"Long story. I've a new mobile phone and a new laptop. The nice man at the tech shop showed me how someone working for Brandon, managed to set up a tracking device on my laptop, my mobile and on my handbag." I sipped the strong mocha made by a disinterested teen named Elsa. I nibbled the gooey chocolate éclair. Just the caffeine and sugar hit I needed once I finished with Oscar at Tech Savy Computers.

"He what?!" Archie spluttered. I heard a clang as he dropped something on the counter. "Sorry, dropped the ice cream scoop, hang on..." I heard Archie giving directions to Pippa as he moved away from the counter. I pictured him headed through the swinging door that led into the kitchen. "Who? How? I mean, I guess Nettie could have, but she's too scatter brained."

I'd considered this question myself and had also concluded Nettie wasn't the likeliest candidate. "Well, it wasn't you, or Eve, I trust her." I prayed my trust wasn't misplaced. "Anyone could have attached a tracker to my things when I was at work. I tend to leave them behind the counter, or on the desk, if I'm working." I paused for another sip, before continuing, "I've a theory. It sounds extremely far-fetched, and will make me sound crazy..." I took another sip of my drink, while I worked out the words in my head.

"Go on," Archie prompted. I could see him, standing over the kitchen sink, running his fingers through his wavy hair, his blue eyes full of concern.

"Brandon, and Gerald are attorneys here in the city. Their business is affiliated with Sinclair Attorneys. In fact, I've just confirmed that *Watson and Kelly Attorney at Law* bought out Sinclair's." I stared at the screen in front of me as I heard Archie gasp. "I think Brandon orchestrated the accidental meeting in the library, and that he set up the fake safety deposit box information from Margo. He saw how well I was doing and knew it wouldn't be long before I started searching for him, and Leo."

"Hmm, weirdly that makes sense, because that information was threatening to send you into a spiral." I heard Archie moving around the small kitchen area at the back of the café. "You're not thinking that Brandon killed Margo, or arranged your parents' death, or..." I sensed the tears in his eyes, as I felt them run down my face.

"I need to contact my aunt and uncle and find out what they know. I'm pretty sure they wouldn't be fooled by Brandon. I'm not staying at the B and B anymore. I'm at a big motel chain on the other side of the city."

"Do you want me to come to you? I can close the café and be there tomorrow." I heard the urgency, the fear in my bestie's voice.

Did I want to see Archie? Yes. "Please don't shut up the café on account of me. I'll be back in West Haven soon. I promise. I decided I don't want to run away and hide in the city after all." I missed Archie, and Eve. A flashing light in the window of a florist gave me an idea. "The sooner I get to the bottom of this, the sooner I'll be back there annoying you," I mustered up every ounce of positivity I could find as I ended our call.

Draining the mocha, I then drank nearly all of the water bottle I'd purchased with my early morning tea. I left the remains of the sweet treat half eaten, Archie's tasted so much better.

The florist offered delivery within the state for a flat rate, if orders were placed by 10am each day. The clock ticked over to 9:45am as I placed two orders for bouquets of chocolates to be delivered. One to Eve at the library, and one to Archie's cafe. No notes or messages to either. It occurred to me that Brandon would've tracked my new location at *The Maple Motel* via my handbag. At least until I ditched it in a bin outside the tech shop. I couldn't worry about that now, I was done with running away every time someone said boo.

At the luggage shop I managed to pick out a similar handbag to my old one. A good brand, fake leather, black, rather than brown, the bag would still fit most of what I lugged to and from work.

I opted for the short taxi ride back to my temporary accommodation. In the guest lounge area, I took advantage of the free Wi-Fi and complimentary glass of water. The first call was to Eve. I let her know I was on track for our meeting the next day. I gave her my new number and new email address, promising to explain in detail during our next call.

My heart pounded in my chest as I dialled Auntie Kris's number. The last time I'd seen my extended family was on my eighteenth birthday. At a sedate dinner at a local restaurant. Uncle Shaun, my dad's brother and Auntie Kris, Mum's sister were as well travelled as my parents. "Hi Auntie Kris, this is Scarlett, Scarlett Nightly," I added, in case there was another Scarlett in Kris's life who called her aunt. "I'm sorry," I didn't know what else to say, as my eyes welled with tears.

"Scarlett, hi! Where are you? Shaun and I are at Tom and Dora's place. We expected to see you here. No one in town knew where you were. Officer Dean told us you worked at the library. A lovely lady, Eve, told us you were out of town indefinitely. Archie, at the café told us the same story. We're worried about you."

I cut her next words off, as tears threatened to form in my eyes. "Before I answer, did Mum and Dad leave a copy of their will with you, or Uncle Shaun?" I found myself crossing my fingers, hoping that the information from Sinclair was all a part of Brandon's elaborate lie.

"Well, yes of course they did. For reasons we are unclear on, they didn't trust the local solicitor and wanted nothing to do with him. They sent us copies of their will, and a letter for you. You do know that they appointed you as executor and that apart from some family items set aside for Shaun and me, that you inherit pretty much everything?"

I thought my heart would pop out of my chest. "So, they are really dead?" I'd been hoping even that was a lie orchestrated by Brandon.

"Oh sweetheart, yes, I'm sorry. A horrible train accident, they wouldn't have suffered. When we couldn't find you, Shaun and I managed to arrange their funeral and cremation overseas. They'll be home for a memorial when you are ready."

I imagined Auntie Kris and Uncle Shaun sitting at the mahogany dining table, important documents spread over the surface, working on bringing my parents home, and trying to locate me. I gulped the lump in my throat away. "I can be home by tomorrow afternoon. I'm in Forest Vale, on a fool's errand. I've a couple of appointments, and I'll catch the coach back tomorrow. I'll ring you when I get in."

"Shaun can meet you at the terminal and bring you home." Auntie Kris's voice broke.

"Thank you both." I felt the familiar sting as my eyes filled with tears. "I promise I'll explain tomorrow," I added. I felt a surge of adrenalin as I hung up the phone. My parents were dead, but they'd not ignored me for their siblings, that counted for something. My aunt and uncle were at my family home, looking for me. Did I think that my family were part of Brandon's elaborate plans? No. Nightlys, and Blys, my mother's maiden name, were stubborn, determined, and trustworthy. At least I hoped that were true. I had to start somewhere, or I'd never reach my goal of bringing Leo home.

Using the motel computer, I looked up *Watson and Kelly Attorneys*. Their business had offices across the state, and some interstate concerns. There'd been speculation of their involvement in corporate crime, though it'd never been proven. It was more difficult to find information about Leo. Official media referred to family without specifying details. Part of me wanted to confront Brandon, the more rational side of me whispered there had to be a better way.

On my way to the elevator, I passed the conference room. The sign on the door told me a child safety officer conference was underway. I my knees buckled as I sank into a lounge chair by the elevator. I opened my laptop and searched child safety officers. I identified a whole government department devoted to child safety, supporting children and their families. The aim of the organisation was to ensure each child's safety and wellbeing.

A chat window popped open asking if I had any questions. I replied that my son was with his father, and I was interested in finding him and gaining custody. Three dots signified the person was typing a response. I found myself holding my breath, waiting for the response.

The chat person asked if I had confirmation the child was mine and explained I could apply for a copy of the birth certificate. I received links to the forms I needed to fill out and told how to lodge them.

I downloaded the forms and saved them on my laptop. I logged into the appropriate department, paid my money and submitted a request for Leo's birth certificate. I contacted the doctor I saw in the city, and the hospital where I gave birth and requested a copy of all relevant information. I also rang the police officer who responded when Leo was stolen and requested a copy of the report. My stomach tied itself in knots, as I waited for the documents to be emailed to my new email address. What if Brandon had managed to erase all evidence of me being pregnant and giving birth? I shuddered at the idea. One by one the documents appeared in my inbox. I opened each one, and saved an additional copy on my device, just in case.

I feel almost lightheaded at the thought we may be reunited one day soon. I dared not hope, but it was a sign from heaven. Maybe your grandparents are working from beyond the grave to make sure I find you. There are so many layers of lies, deception, broken promises, and shattered vows, I feel like at last, I am strong enough to unravel them all.

Chapter Sixteen

A yawn escaped my lips. The lack of sleep the previous evening was rapidly catching up. I closed the internet search, collected my things, tucking them back into my handbag and headed up to my room. I put a Do Not Disturb sign on my door. In case I slept, though I didn't expect to. Every time I closed my eyes, visions of my parents, and Leo, standing far away from me, just out of reach, taunted my half dreams.

Drenched in sweat, when I finally got out from under the covers the digital clock told me it was midday. I hadn't been asleep for long. I needed exercise, and food, but firstly, a nice, long, hot shower. I loved that the motel provided toiletries as well as fluffy towels and robes. Wearing the leggings and another t-shirt from the supermarket back home, I opted for a brisk walk around the local area. I passed the shop where I'd replaced my tech less than twenty minutes into my walk. The digital sign on the top of a bus identified their next stop would take me near Brandon's office. For a spilt second, I considered it. Arriving by bus, yelling at the bully, in his business environment, to return my son to me. Nothing about that scene screamed success.

With a spring in my step, I remembered the child safety centre, and their helpful online help. I smiled as I checked that my new emails still included the evidence that I gave birth to Leo, and that Brandon took him from the hospital. I could play the long game, waiting, until I had all my ducks in a row. The trickiest part would be ensuring we were safe from anything else Brandon could throw at us. I marched past the bus, and the plethora of takeaway convenience stores in a wide circle, back to the motel.

The restaurant, still serving lunch, won me over with baked potato with bacon, cheese and slaw. I splurged on non-alcoholic ginger beer, and a side salad. I salivated over the delicious different tastes and textures. Maybe I'd learn to cook, simple things like this, when I returned home.

An hour later, as I headed towards the lift, I saw a familiar face at reception. I ducked behind a glittery poster advertising a local karaoke night. I watched, unable to hear their words, as Brandon stood over the counter, his face inches from Tim. Luckily, I'd provided a false name when I booked in the previous evening. I'd mentioned to Tim that I was worried about an ex stalking me and that I'd appreciate it if anyone came asking, that the motel didn't reveal my whereabouts.

I slid into the elevator as it opened, as much as I wanted to watch the rest of the conversation I didn't want to be caught by my nemesis. The phone in my room was ringing as I opened the door. I crashed onto the bed, picking up the receiver. "Hello, Miss MacDonald, it's Tim at reception. A man named Brandon Kelly, just came here looking for a Miss Scarlett Nightly. I told him clearly that we had no one by that name, or anyone who looked anything like the woman he described, staying here. I thought you should know."

"Thank you." I replaced the receiver in its cradle and rolled on to my back. *Knowledge is power* someone famous once said. They were right. Brandon was far less intimidating when I had the upper hand.

I sent an email to the B and B, asking for a refund, apologising for leaving abruptly, citing a family emergency. The email bounced back, unable to be delivered. I tried to find the site where I booked initially and was unable to find any trace of the bed and breakfast accommodation run by Eliza and Cora. On a hunch I looked at the staff page of Brandon's law firm, and found Eliza listed as office manager. Damn.

The Sinclair Attorney website appeared to be under construction. I rang the number in my phone for Mr Sinclair. The number was disconnected, with no voice message or redirection. I decided against messaging Eve and Archie to be careful. No more jumping at shadows. Brandon would not win. This required all the stubbornness and determination I possessed. I also needed focus, concentration, and cunning.

The Watson family were entrepreneurs, well known, generational old money. I knew about the book on their achievements; we kept a copy at the library. My intuition told me there'd be an internet presence. The Watson Family website proved a useful tool. Outlining their farming history, how they branched into real estate, and law. Gerald's nephew worked in the medical research field. The Watsons donated to several local and international organisations. The Kelly name entwined with the Watson's for a couple of generations. I found no mention of my family being related to them in any way. Nightlys and Blys weren't originally from West Haven. My parents moved when they were married while my father built his practise and my mother established her art school.

After a second attempt to contact Sinclair Attorneys, I filled out a generic form on the legal services commission website, reporting them for suspected fraudulent behaviour. My medical studies had included a couple of subjects pertaining to law. It seemed prudent to know the legal ramifications of providing patient care. Honestly, that part scared me more than the actual doctoring.

A search on a couple of national and international news sites confirmed the train accident and subsequent death of twenty passengers, including two Australian tourists. Hot tears trickled down my cheeks as I read the account of the train that derailed and plummeted down a steep ravine, on a scenic tourist trip between two towns with unpronounceable names. The local authorities were investigating the accident. Closing the site, I'd read all that I needed to. I stretched, and boiled the kettle, adding a coffee bag to the tiny motel cup. I drained the cup in two gulps, grateful for the caffeine hit.

After splashing water on my face, I returned to the little table and reopened my computer. The tech guy transferred my files, documents and photos. I smiled at the picture of baby Leo. *I'll never stop trying to find you. I'll be smarter about it, I understand it might be a while, but we will be together one day.* I managed to keep my eyes dry as I reflected on my next steps.

When I'd left the sisters, I left behind the book on Empaths. They were pushing the narrative of me being different, helpless, a mess, and now I understood why. Brandon's agenda, to keep me unsettled, unfit, unsure. Still, something about being an empath rang true. With a discerning eye and being aware of the dodgy websites, I established that alongside empathy, some people exhibited empath tendencies. The traits of an empath that resonated with me were the ability to pick up on the emotions and moods of people around me. It explained my aversion to crowds. There was debate over whether the ability is passed through family lines or random. It was heartening to know I wasn't crazy, when I felt out of sorts, grumpy, sad, even sick, for no apparent reason.

More knowledge – more power.

I felt a burning desire to read my own tarot cards. Having lost mine to the explosion I tucked my laptop and mobile into my bag and headed out. Tim gave me the thumbs up as I left, which I hoped meant Brandon was no longer lurking. Did I see a bookstore at the shopping centre? With each step towards the shops, I told myself – *I can do this.*

The Book Shelf was located in between the chemist and the donut shop. It boasted a wide range of indie and traditionally published books, craft sets and new age incidentals, including tarot cards. I chose a set with a lunar theme. I picked up a couple of other bargains, including a children's book I'd love to read to Leo.

Knowledge is power, so is positivity and planning ahead. I'm biding my time, planning the day when I get to finally bring you home.

AS I LEFT THE CENTRE on my way back to the motel, I passed a taxi waiting in line for a fare. I opted to not walk back, after so many steps the last few days my legs ached at the thought of adding more. The driver wasn't chatty, which allowed me time to think about what question I wanted to ask my new cards.

"Will you be dining in the restaurant?" Tim enquired as I entered the foyer.

Keen to get my tarot cards out, plus there was a chance that Brandon would send someone into the restaurant to spy in case I were here. "I'm going to order room service, it's been a big day, and I'll be checking out tomorrow."

Tim nodded, his best customer service smile on his face. "I hope you found everything to your satisfaction," he said. "Just dial five to place your meal order, on the telephone in your room. You can order drinks and dessert too. If you need a taxi tomorrow morning, you could consider booking this evening." He handed me a business card with the name of a local taxi service. I took the card, and thanked him, wondering if there were any way Brandon would know if I pre-booked a taxi.

The butterflies in my stomach reminded me I'd be returning home tomorrow. To my family home, without my parents, or my son. I was keen to see Archie and Eve. The Book Week activities were another positive, I loved my job. I was looking forward to seeing my aunt and uncle.

The room service menu was on the table beside the bed. I chose finger food. Little spring rolls, celery and carrots with an assortment of dips, and a large apple juice. I ordered a strong coffee and a chocolate cake with ice cream for dessert, ordering it to arrive an hour after the main course.

When I switched computers, I needed to keep my old email address, to keep track of bills, until I could change my contact details. I checked my emails, not surprised to find an anonymous threatening email *Beware, you were warned,* I reported it as spam and deleted it. I followed the same process for the next five threatening emails. Deleted and reported each one. I wasn't certain but I hoped he knew I was deleting them unread.

Shuffling my tarot cards proved to be a calming exercise. I turned each card over, studying the picture, listening to the words that popped into my head. The cards comprised suits, and royal cards, like any deck. Some of the pictures resonated more than others. The images on swords and wands made me shudder. The pentagrams and cups felt lighter. The ladies depicted on the four queens held me enthralled. *Safe, strong, confident, motherly, protected,* words popped into my head, until a knock at the door drew me back to reality.

The waiter left the tray of food on the table. I thanked him, and moved the cards to the side table, lest I spill any food on them. I hesitated, before returning them to their box. *Don't be silly Scarlett, you can draw them out again after dinner.* I told myself as I turned on the television, delighted to find reruns of my favourite British crime show.

The spring rolls were first, then the dips and vegetables and finally the crunchy apple. Archie would be impressed with my food choices, and that I was thinking of writing a list of recipes to try at home. More than that, I wanted to create a weekly menu plan, including options like this, and challenging myself with more complicated fare, like baked potatoes, or maybe lasagne.

My tarot cards forgotten I googled easy recipes, opened a new document on my laptop and started writing. I'd forgotten about dessert and when the waiter knocked at the door, it startled me. *Don't be ridiculous Scarlett, it's the waiter, not some evil bully.* I admonished myself as I peered through the eye hole in the door.

Archie rang. I filled him in on the key news from my day and listened to his news while I polished off the last of the cake and ice cream. "I've been talking to Eve, and I hope you don't mind, but we've put together a hamper for your aunt and uncle. We're about to meet, to deliver it together. We won't tell them any details about Brandon or Leo, that's up to you to share. We just wanted to welcome them back to town and offer our condolences."

My heart jumped at the kindness and love of my friends. "Thank you, and please thank Eve as well. I think that's a lovely idea. I don't mind if you tell them a little about what happened, depending on if you feel it's appropriate. I trust you, and Eve, and Kris and Shaun too, I guess. I should trust that my parents trusted them." My stomach rumbled as nervous energy competed with the cake. "I'll see you tomorrow." I found myself smiling at the thought.

Should I have suggested to Archie that they should be wary, that being connected to me put them in danger? That was my old way of thinking. There may be a threat but worry about that wasn't going to solve anything. Moving forward, I'd make an official application for custody. Change my approach so we were safe from harm. The only problem was, I hadn't quite figured out how I was going to achieve that.

Chapter Seventeen

After the best night's sleep that I attributed to the four cards under my pillow, I carefully packed the Queens into their box. Was the lack of nightmares due to the cards under my pillow, or because I'd chosen not to be intimidated? Packing my belongings into the purple suitcase didn't take long. I handed my key in at reception and waited for the taxi.

The taxi driver agreed to drive past Waston and Kellys attorneys. A red brick two storey semi-detached with their name blazoned on a board at of the front building. Dedicated parking spaces out the front. Pretentious. I wasn't sure what else I expected to see. Maybe Eliza, Gerald, or Brandon standing out the front.

My coach to West Haven wasn't due for another hour, so after paying the taxi driver, I went in search of a coffee. I didn't have to walk far. The Café in the coach terminal offered a coffee and a choc muffin. Not as good as Archie's, but I needed food in my stomach. Two older men with suitcases shuffled in and sat down at the table next to me. One of the men hobbled to the counter and placed their order. A couple of teenagers in torn black jeans and white shirts sat across from me, tucking their backpacks under their chairs. A woman tugging a suitcase beside her, perched on a stool at the counter at the side of café.

Taking a deep breath, I tried switching on my intuition. I'd read something about balance. I didn't have to be all logic or all woo woo, life could be a mix of both. Logic told me it would be unlikely any of my fellow customers would be reporting back to Brandon. Intuition agreed, unless Brandon sent someone to sit here all day waiting for me to turn up.

A coach pulled into a space right outside the doors. A large white modern vehicle with its name emblazoned in large blue font along the side. The other occupants in the café finished their food and started collecting their belongings. I waited, watching each patron. Eventually, I deposited my plate and cup onto the tray and headed towards the glass doors. Reluctantly I handed my purple bag to the driver. *It'll be safe,* I told myself as he placed it with all the other luggage in the side compartment of the bus.

The coach wasn't full. About half of the forty seats were taken, leaving a random criss-cross pattern of seats to choose from. I opted for one of the spots at the front of the bus. The position just behind the driver. I moved into the thick deep blue material cushioned bench, grateful to have both spots to myself. Positioning myself against the window, I placed my handbag on the aisle seat, taking out one of the books I bought to read during my sabbatical.

Whether it was the book, or the rhythm of the coach, I must've nodded off. I woke with a start, confused about where I was. As my brain worked through the fog, slowly I realised I was safe and on my way home.

One step closer to finding you and bringing you home. I'll do it properly. I told Leo. *There's so much about West Haven I want to show you. Archie, Eve, Kris, and Shaun will love you, as much as I do.*

After a couple of stops in suburbia, less than ten passengers remained on the coach as we approached West Haven. As we got closer, I sent a text to Archie and Eve that my uncle would be picking me up. I messaged Auntie Kris my expected arrival time. My heart leapt at the thought of seeing them. I looked forward to the routine of work, being productive, and getting Book Week organised.

THOUGH I HADN'T SEEN my relatives for years, I recognised my uncle instantly. Shaun was nearly as tall as his brother Tom, my father. It was oddly comforting seeing him standing by his black jeep, waiting for me. He enveloped me in a bear hug. "It's so good to see you, Scarlett."

Tears trickled down my face as we drove into the driveway. The grey washed brick façade of my childhood home brought back memories that scrolled through my brain like a *this is your life* movie reel. Roses and geraniums grew amongst the older bushes and tall trees bordering the block. Standing on the top step ready to greet us, my Auntie Kris was tiny in comparison to my uncle. A little shorter than my mum, at five-foot-eight I was taller than most of my female ancestors. Both my relatives had reddish tinges in their now greying hair. Uncle Shaun's hair was short; Auntie Kris's long hair was tied back with a black ribbon. I hopped from the jeep and embraced my aunt.

"It's so good to see you Scarlett," Auntie Kris said as she led me into the formal lounge room. Mum and Dad bought the house when I was a baby. Originally it was a project they planned to renovate together. I remembered the builders, plumbers, and electricians who assisted with the various projects throughout the years. Home. I drew in a breath as I took in my surroundings.

Being in the house where I grew up, sitting at the dining room table with Uncle Shaun and Auntie Kris made things more real, and less weird than I imagined. A huge part of me hoped I'd find my parents at the table when I walked through the door. The disappointment at their empty seats hit me like a punch to my gut.

The black and white tablecloth lay across half the table, the other half laid bare, with two neat piles of paper. A tray with three cups of coffee waited on the tablecloth. Aunt Kris reached across and squeezed my hand. "There's so much we don't understand." She swept her arm to include Uncle Shaun in her statement. "Your parents were organised, even in death, or before their death," her voice shook. "They sent us letters, and one for you, to be opened on the unlikely event that they both died together." She passed an unopened envelope across the table to me.

I eyed it sceptically. The last few documents I read ended up being lies. I wasn't in a hurry to open this one. Even if the letter was from my dead parents.

"Aren't you going to read it?" Auntie Kris asked softly.

Shaking my head, I stared at the others at the table. "I can't, not yet. In the last couple of weeks, I've been fed information about me and my family, and it's all turned out to be cruel, horrible lies. When I returned home, asking for help, my parents appeared disinterested, too busy to help. I can't go down another rabbit hole of lies and deceit. I love my parents, and the both of you, but I need to be strong, for Leo and for myself." I picked the mug with the strong black coffee a sipped it slowly. As a teen I'd always drunk it black. It was sweet of Auntie Kris to remember.

Auntie Kris looked at Uncle Shaun. He gave an ever so slight nod of his head. "Do you trust us, Scarlett?" she asked. "Do you trust your parents loved you?"

I sighed. Despite the hurt, the anger, the angst, and overwhelming anxiety, I loved my parents. Although I didn't understand their reasons, I knew they loved me and thought they were doing their best for me. Shaun and Kris had joined us to celebrate Christmases, birthdays and other celebrations for as long as I could remember. They always asked me about my hobbies, spent time being interested in their only niece. Neither were married or had children of their own. "I do trust you, and my parents, even if I don't understand their motivations."

My aunt reached her hand across the table, gently touching mine. "You know a lot of this story already. Your mum and I moved to West Haven as young adults, from Forest Vale. We thought we'd stay a few months, learn some arty stuff, have some fun then move back to the city. We both ended up staying, for different reasons."

I'd heard this story before. "West Haven was known in the city as a town for artists, sculptors, creative types, to come and learn their trade. A couple of well-known artists lived here." I tried to remember the story told to me a long time ago.

Uncle Shaun took up the story. "Your dad and I moved here with our parents when we were teens. We'd planned to move to the city first chance we got. Instead, your dad fell in love with your mum, and I, well I decided here was as good as any for a base during my travels. Like all small towns, there are gossips, good guys, and bad guys. The Watsons are rich and like to think of themselves as generous. The Kellys are the poor cousins of the Watsons. They spend a lot of time in and out of gaol."

"For whatever reason, Wendy and Will Kelly hated your parents. Your parents were successful, happy, all the things they weren't. The Kellys spent years in and out of gaol. Brandon went to live with his cousin, Gerald Watson." Auntie Kris gulped back a sob. "Gerald knew how to charm people, make them believe him, then con, steal, take, everything from them." I wondered if Gerald had hurt or conned Auntie Kris, the venom in her voice made it sound personal. I didn't feel right asking for more information.

Uncle Shaun's eyes filled with tears. "Brandon turned into a bully. We didn't know he'd found you, and about Leo, until you got home...afterwards. You parents were worried about you and wanted so badly to help you get Leo back. They were terrified that Brandon would hurt Leo, or you." He looked at Kris, then to me. "We didn't know any of this, until we received letters from them, a couple of days after they died."

Tears ran down my cheeks. How could life have treated us this way? My parents always helped others, and their brother and sister were good people. I breathed in, exhaling slowly, willing the tears to stop.

Now wasn't the time to fall apart. I sipped my coffee, watching my aunt and uncle as they eyed me, the worry, concern and grief evident in their eyes. "I'm not sure how much Archie and Eve told you, but you know about Leo. Brandon stealing him triggered an anxiety induced PTSD or something like that. It took me three years to heal enough to find and keep the amazing job I have at the library. Brandon must have been keeping tabs on me, realised I'd be strong enough to fight for Leo and started a series of events aimed at breaking me." I glanced around the room. The black and white lounge and matching reading armchairs, the side tables, the plush red rug on the thick off-white carpet. The room hadn't changed much in the ten years since I'd lived there. On the white shelf, books by my parents' favourite authors were nestled alongside photos of their travels and family shots. "He nearly succeeded. I started down a rabbit warren, looking for Brandon and Leo, being buffeted here and there with all the drama he threw at me."

Auntie Kris's hand touched mine. "And now?" she asked gently.

"Now I'm ready to fight. I'm going to contact children's safety services and find the proper channels to fight for Leo. My plan must be perfect. It might take longer than I'd hoped, but I will get Leo back. The first step is protecting those I care about here, before Brandon can cause any more harm." I looked from Kris to Shaun. "The two of you, Archie, and Eve are the four people who mean the world to me. I need to ensure you are safe."

Uncle Shaun stood up suddenly. "How do we stop Brandon?" He started pacing the room. "If he managed to kill Tom and Dora, how do we protect ourselves?"

"I've been thinking about that. He only started his campaign to terrorise me, when he thought I was getting stronger and might be about to fight for Leo. He thought he'd scare me back into the mess I was when he first stole my child." I pulled out my laptop and pulled up my emails. "I've collected the forms I need and received information from the hospital and the police station where I reported Leo missing. Brandon hadn't the chance to doctor those records."

Shaun returned to his seat. "Are you thinking he'll stop terrorising you if he knows you'll fight back?"

"I'm hoping that's the case. I've already replaced my phone, computer and handbag, because he managed to bug them." I peered into the bottom of my coffee mug. "Is there any chance of another coffee?"

A COUPLE OF HOURS LATER, and it felt like I'd never left West Haven. Archie called in after work, with a selection of salads, rolls, cold meats, and cheeses. "I'm still a little disappointed in the way my parents chose to protect Leo and me. I do understand a little better, which helps." I said quietly as I poured four glasses of water.

Uncle Shaun had been quiet during dinner. Like my father, he preferred to think through all his options before speaking. "I can only stay in town for a few days, until after the memorial. But if you need anything, at any time of the day or night, just message or ring me and if I can't be here, I'll send someone."

If I ever knew exactly what Uncle Shaun did for a living, I'd forgotten. Construction maybe, or project management. "Thank you, Uncle Shaun." I smiled at the man who reminded me so much of my father.

"Unfortunately, I'll have to leave after the service too." Auntie Kris's eyes glistened with unshed tears. "The school could only find someone to replace me for a week. I'm only a couple of hours away, so if you need anything, let me know. I'll help where I can."

I nodded my thanks, overwhelmed by all the offers of support.

Archie passed the fruit and nut platter to Uncle Shaun. "Despite her protestations, Scarlett has me, and I do my best to look after her. Not that she's hard work." He rolled his eyes for dramatic effect.

I glanced around the table. Sitting here with three people I loved, I was reminded of the loss of my parents. "It's so easy to lose touch with those we care about. Can we try to meet for a meal once a month? In honour of my parents." I didn't know whether it was okay to ask that, but it sounded like something families did. I wanted to start making connections, putting down roots, forming a community, for Leo and myself.

"That's a lovely idea, yes," Auntie Kris said, as a tear ran down her cheek.

Uncle Shaun's voice sounded gruff, as he held back his emotions. "Give me some dates and I'll make sure my work schedule fits around our monthly family get togethers."

Archie raised his hand. "I'm in too, if I'm invited that is," he said, lightening the mood.

"Of course you're invited. You're my best friend. West Haven wouldn't be home without you," I said, dry eyed for the first time since I arrived home. Through the dining room window, I noticed the evening sky was dotted with stars. A reddish hue lingered, just above the horizon. It could have been any evening meal with my parents, except it wasn't.

"Are you going to live here, by yourself?" Archie asked me, as he passed the bowl of salad from me to Shaun. "Sorry, I didn't mean to sound insensitive."

I smiled at my best friend. "You can ask me anything, and I'll answer as best I can." I wasn't just referring to his question now, and he knew that. He kept me sane, grounded, and I owed him my life. My eyes caught Auntie Kris's. "Apparently yes, the house is mine, one hundred percent. It's huge, but I'll get used to it. Also, it means I don't have to find somewhere else to live." I managed a weak smile.

"Kris and I are only a telephone call away if Scarlett needs anything. Archie, please contact either of us if we can assist in any way. We all know you value your independence Scarlett, but asking for help isn't a sign of weakness, and we want you to know that." Uncle Shaun held up a half empty bottle of lemonade, "Now, would anyone like another drink before coffee and ice cream?"

SLEEPING IN THE BED I'd slept in as a child and a teenager felt more than a little weird. In the back of my mind, I heard my parents' voices –

Don't stay up reading too long
Light's out before midnight
Make your bed every morning, no matter how you slept or how busy you are
Don't leave clothes on the floor

Like a video on silent play, I saw younger versions of myself, and my parents. Memories of reading together, sitting and talking, working on homework.

Physically the room was still the same. My single bed lay against the wall under the window. A thick multi-coloured woollen blanket lay over the pink doona and thinner blankets. Pale pink and blue pillowcases and an old teddy bear I'd owned for as long as I could remember waited for me. "Hi Mr Ted," I whispered as I sat on the edge of my bed. Gingerly picking him up, I patted his soft fur. "I wish you could talk, but I know you're a good listener, so I'll tell you my story, later." Tears ran down my cheeks as I placed Mr Ted back on the pillow. My old wooden desk still held the fruit tin I'd decorated as a receptacle for my pens and pencils. Even its contents were the same. A couple of exercise books, covered in brown paper and labelled Scarlett Nightly were at the back of the piece of furniture. Next to the desk stood the bookshelf. All my favourite childhood books were there. Alongside the books were couple of jigsaw puzzles and board games I used to play. Opening the cupboard I half expected to see my old clothes hanging where I left them, over ten years ago.

The boxes labelled with my name surprised me. I opened the smaller one on top of the stack. I felt the blood rush through my veins as I read the note on top of the pile of baby clothes. *Scarlett, and Leo, we wish we could have welcomed you home with love and spoilt you with this collection of items. It was such fun collecting these for you. We hope there is a happy ending to your story, and that we are able to welcome you home soon. All our love Mum and Dad xxx*

I folded the note, closed the box and the wardrobe, and started counting backwards from one hundred, purposely slowing my breathing. Unlike my cottage, this house was huge, I counted my steps as I paced to the kitchen. The kettle on I scooped a generous amount of hot chocolate into my mug. The house was quiet. Shaun and Kris opted to stay overnight at their own homes. Neither one rented out their West Haven houses, and they thought they might clean and tidy them while they were here. I took my mug to the dining room table. The envelope addressed to me was sitting innocently amongst the papers. Although I looked everywhere else, as I sipped my warm drink, my eyes kept coming back to the innocent looking envelope. If it were anything like the other note I found...

Just rip the band-aid off Scarlett

I tore open the envelope.

Dearest Scarlett, We're sorry...for everything. Even now, if you are reading this, we can't tell you everything you want to know or want to hear. Please believe we love you, and we never meant to hurt you. The pain in your eyes was unbearable, but we honestly thought we were doing the best we could to keep you, and Leo safe. We should have helped you stand up to Brandon. We'll always regret that.

We don't have the answers, but we know you can find the solution. Take a step back, think of it as one of the puzzles you loved so much as a child. You can do this. We love you, always, and are so proud of the woman you've become.

There is so much more we wanted to tell you, but we needed to keep you safe from harm. We watched as Archie cared for you. We silently cheered when you started to heal. Your job at the library made us so proud.

One day you'll find Leo and bring him home. We are sure you will achieve that, as you've achieved everything else you've put your mind to. Never stop believing in yourself Scarlett. You're stronger than you give yourself credit for.

We love you, always have, always will, to the moon and the stars and back.

Mum and Dad xxx

Chapter Eighteen

I made my morning coffee, in the silence of the large kitchen. The magpies warbled their morning song just outside the window. Kris, Shaun, and Archie all offered to bring breakfast to the house. I declined their offers. I had to get used to the quiet eventually.

The walk to work was longer than the trip from my cottage. Did I need a car? Both my parents' cars were in the garage under the house. That would mean getting over my fear of driving. Walking would be fine for now. Driving was a challenge for another day.

Only a few days ago, I thought I'd be away from work for weeks, maybe longer. There was still so much to sort out, with my parents' estate, and starting the process to bring Leo home. I needed normalcy and routine back into my life. As I arrived at the back door at the same time as Eve, I found myself smiling. "Good morning, Eve." I held out my hand, helping her with her bags, so she could easily unlock the door.

My boss beamed back. "It's so good to see you!" She swept me up in a hug, complete with the various bags we both held. "I've added extra security since you were here last. I'll give you the new keys and security protocol over breakfast."

Before I could ask 'what breakfast' I heard footsteps approaching. I swung around as I heard Archie say, "Breakfast, as ordered. I added a couple of extra treats for morning tea. It's so great to have Scarlett back, and Eve, I appreciate that you are keeping her occupied and out of trouble," he winked. "Will I follow you in and pop these somewhere?" He eyed the bags. "It looks like you have your hands full."

"That would be lovely Archie, thank you," Eve replied. "On the table in the kitchenette please and thank you for the extra goodies." Eve led us inside and locked the door firmly behind us.

I followed Archie to the kitchen while he deposited our delicious smelling breakfast onto the table. "Are you staying for breakfast?" I realised I missed Archie more than I thought, and not just in a platonic, friendship only way. I'd declined his offer to stay the night in the big house to protect me, yet my heart skipped a little every time I saw him.

"Pippa has to be at school by 9am, so I'd better get back there. She's been a godsend." Archie paused, I could tell he wanted to say more. "I'm embarrassed to admit, she's been so keen to work, I was worried she may be related to Brandon somehow. I checked into her family. I can't find any connection to the Kellys or Watsons. Her family moved here for work at the local community college, both parents are teachers. Her dad teaches technical drawing and her mum's a cooking teacher. They used to manage a farm."

The urge to hug Archie, for the depths he went to, to make sure I was safe, was overwhelming. I compromised with a quick squeeze of his hand. "Thank you. I guess we'll have to work out the balance between too trusting and too cynical,"

"I might be able to help you with that," Eve joined us in the kitchen. "Beth can fill you in, but I've an idea on how we may be able to discover truthful information on suspects, er, individuals, if we need to." Her cheeks turned a rosy, red colour as she quickly changed the subject. "I'll let you out the front door. I'm sure we'll be seeing you again soon."

While Eve and Archie walked out the front of the library, I unpacked our breakfast. Not only had Archie packed us coffees, a water bottle each, ham and cheese toasties and hazelnut croissants, there were a selection of macaroons and mini chocolate muffins for later. The warm feeling in my chest was not something I'd felt in such a long time. Could it be that being back in West Haven with Kris, Shaun, Archie, and Eve helped heal my anxiety? *Home...back where I belonged*...whether it was my intuition or logic talking I couldn't tell. I wasn't scared or feeling the need to run away. I found myself looking forward to whatever the day would bring.

Eve returned, a large smile on her face. "It's so good to have you back Scarlett. We've time to eat, before we open. There's so much to talk about. Let's start with our main project. I've a approached a few authors to come along to our festivities. A week-long celebration of authors and reading. Some writing workshops and writing competitions for all ages. I love your ideas, and I've some of my own as well. After we eat, we can swap notes." She picked up a triangle sandwich and took a bite. I did the same, savouring the flavours. Takeaways in the city just didn't live up to Archie's cooking.

The sweet and bitter flavours of the mocha, I'd missed more than I'd care to admit. "I learnt a couple of important lessons during my few days away." I spoke firmly, buoyed by the feeling of home. "No one makes café food better than Archie," I grinned. "Also, most of what I thought to be true, isn't. I'm sick of letting bullies push me around and intimidate me. It's time to fight back."

My boss sipped from her takeaway cup. "It's so easy to create misinformation and lies. Not so easy to sift through it to find the truth." She eyed me as she picked up a second triangle. "I mentioned I knew a way to find the truth. I know a person who may be able to help. He goes by the name Rosso. No last name. He's a tech genius, whose only interest is in uncovering the truth. Any truth. He doesn't do it for the money, but money is always appreciated. I trust him explicitly for reasons I may tell you one day. We've been friends for a long time."

"If you trust him, that would be amazing. I'm willing to pay, a reasonable amount. If I can be assured that I have the truth and not an adulterated Brandon version, then I have power. Power over Brandon, and no longer powerless against him." I sipped the mocha, wishing it were a bottomless cup. I'd never get sick of the flavour burst.

Before we could discuss more, someone started banging on the front door.

"IT'S OKAY MR EVANS we were about to open the library. We open at 9am." Eve smiled at one of our older patrons, as she unlocked the doors and allowed him in a few minutes early. Since losing his wife, Mr Evans was a daily visitor, spending hours sitting in a comfy chair reading. Eve gently directed him towards the front counter to return the books he held. I checked the door, put out our sign, and placed the welcome mat outside the door. As I concentrated on my breathing, my heart slowly returned to its normal beat. The pounding on the door had set my pulse racing, imagining Brandon on the other side.

I laughed at myself, letting my mind get carried away. At least this time, I managed to catch my anxiety before it took over. A positive start to my return. I even managed a smile as Nettie swaggered into the library, staring at me as she did a circuit of the room before heading back towards the main street. I swallowed the fear that bubbled in my stomach. I was home, in my comfort zone. My town, my workplace. Not Brandon's.

The butterflies settled down. I turned, as Eve touched my arm. "Are you okay?"

"Yes, that was Nettie. She's a little crazy, but also, she's one of the people Brandon has working for him. I think she's the one who spilt paint on the books, but I can't be certain." I picked up a couple of books sitting on the front counter. "I'll check the overnight returns chute if you like."

"Sounds good, and I'll help Mr Evans and keep an eye out for Nettie. I've a feeling we'll be seeing more of her." Eve nodded towards our early morning customer. "Once you come back, can you stay around the counter, I've got some admin to catch up on, now you've returned."

"Sure thing boss," I grinned. "Seriously, thanks so much, for everything. I appreciate you letting me take leave and welcoming me back, working here is awesome."

I sorted the returns, ready for shelving later in the day. A steady stream of customers walked through the door, smiling as I greeted them. "I'm so glad you're back dear," Mrs Oddy patted my arm. "Do you have any new thrillers? I've finished the last three you recommended." Even with her grey hair wound up into a high bun, she stood less than five feet tall.

Her friend, Miss Carey stood only a little taller. Her grey hair plaited into pigtails that hung down her back. "I'm after some of those cozy mystery books please, and a book to remind me how to crochet."

"What a good idea," Mrs Oddy agreed, "I'd like to learn knitting too, if you have a book handy."

"If it's not too much trouble," Miss Carey added.

My heart felt full, knowing I could help my customers. "It's not too much trouble at all, come this way ladies." I led the septuagenarians to the popular fiction section.

I left Sadie and Gertrude, as they insisted I call them, to flick through some books, and returned to the counter. A couple of men in suits entered the library. "Can I help you find a book?" I asked them as they approached the counter.

"We're looking for Scarlett Nightly," the taller of the two spoke in a deep gravelly voice.

"You've found her," I replied. "How can I help?"

"We're from the insurance company, on behalf the owner of the house you were renting. We want to ask you some questions about the explosion and fire. There's money to be paid to the owners," the stockier man spoke as he referred to his tablet.

"May I see some identification please." I held out my hand for a business card. The two men looked at each other, patted their pockets, as if searching for their wallets.

Referring to his tablet, the shorter man repeated, "We need to ask you some questions, and there's the matter of compensation."

Neither man appeared willing to provide me identification. I doubted they were legitimately from the insurance company. A light bulb went on in my brain. "You need to speak to Officer Dean at the police station. He and the fire department confirmed the explosion was not my fault. I believe someone started it deliberately. Can I have your names, so I can let him know you'll be calling in."

The men looked at each other. The taller one, who spoke first, took his mobile from his pocket, and spoke, even though I'd not heard it ring. "Yes, we'll be right there." With a curt nod at me, he turned and left the library, the other man following closely behind him.

Chalk up another victory to me. I knew instinctively that Brandon was behind the visitors. Trying to harass me, to throw me into a panic.

My laptop lay open at the counter. I started a new word document. With today's date at the top, I listed the visit from Nettie, and the two men, supposedly from the insurance company.

Eve joined me behind the counter. "Is everything okay?"

"Yes, I'm just keeping track of things that happen, time and dates that sort of thing. In case I need to make complaint to the police. Do you know Officer Dean well? Is he trustworthy?"

Eve's cheeks reddened. "Eddie and I have been out a couple of times, for dinner, and a movie. Originally from up north, he moved here a few years ago. Prefers the peace and quiet to the city. He's decent, honest. I trust him. We're not formally dating." She fiddled with the beaded bracelet she always wore on her left wrist. "It must be time for morning tea."

Chapter Nineteen

The rest of the morning proved to be uneventful. I spent the time at the counter, assisting patrons, while Eve caught up on chores in the office. Before I'd a chance to consider a supermarket visit to grab lunch, Archie arrived with chicken wraps for Eve and me.

"Don't think this will be a daily occurrence," he said pretending to frown. "It's just that I know you've not had a chance to stock your fridge yet. I may have given a hint to Kris and Shaun, that you often forget to eat, so check if they've filled your fridge before you go shopping." He turned on his way out and added, "I may have also suggested driving lessons, so don't be surprised if Shaun offers." Archie slipped through the door as a couple of patrons entered. I didn't know whether I wanted to thank him, kiss him or yell at him. Throw my arms around him probably.

I showed the young woman dressed in jogging gear where to find the health section, and the gentleman with the walking stick where to find his favourite author. I ducked my head into the office to tell Eve lunch was ready on the kitchen table. She offered to mind the counter while I ate first. As I bit into the chicken wrap, with just the right amount of salad and no mayo, my toes curled in their shoes as I thought about driving.

My parents had two vehicles. Mum's old van she used to take her artwork to exhibits and workshops, and Dad's jeep. Not one of the newer editions, his old jalopy had character. Both were a lot bigger than anything I'd driven, since I learnt to drive in the jeep, more than ten years ago.

Don't let emotions stop you Scarlett, I told myself. I needed to drive, now that I lived that little bit further away from work and the shops. Lugging groceries home wouldn't be practical and I didn't fancy taking a taxi everywhere. I sighed, as I boiled the kettle for a coffee. *Don't overthink it, you can do it.*

The next unusual event occurred as we prepared to close at the end of the day. A courier dropped a small parcel at the counter. "Excuse me," I called after the young man with the bicycle helmet, and lycra leggings, "Where did this come from?" I held up the parcel with my name on it.

He shrugged. "No idea. I picked it up at the depot on Middle Street. You could ring and ask them, if there's no return address, or note inside."

The courier left. I opened the package. It was empty. I pulled the bubble wrap apart; in case I'd discarded the item accidentally. "Why go to all the trouble of sending an empty package?" I mused aloud.

"Do you want me to call Eddie?" Eve asked, holding her mobile phone.

"I don't think so. I'm just going to ignore it. Brandon's just trying to scare me with message about there's nothing I can do, or some such nonsense." I hoped I sounded braver than I felt.

Eve eyed me suspiciously. "What do you think Archie will have to say about that?"

"I'll talk to him tonight. He's coming to my parent's house, er my house, for dinner. I'd love you to see my aunt and uncle again before they leave, would you like to come to dinner tomorrow night?"

"That would be lovely, and good change of subject," Eve pretended to frown. "I know you'll do the right thing. Now, let's get out of here, it's past home time."

I WALKED AROUND THE back towards the kitchen and found Uncle Shaun and Archie chatting over the barbeque. Uncle Shaun turned to me, "I hope you don't mind but I've set up security cameras around the property, added extra locks to all the windows and doors, and if you agree, I'll set up an alarm system as well."

I couldn't help smiling. Putting my bags on the outdoor table, I gave my uncle a hug, careful not to knock the barbeque tongs out of his hand. "Thank you, you're amazing." I let go just as quickly, as the heat from the hot plate radiated out towards my sleeve.

Auntie Kris walked through the back door carrying a tray with salad and bread rolls. "Hi Scarlett, let's sit down and let the men cook." I moved my bags out of the way and joined her at the table. "The kitchen cupboards and fridge are fully stocked, I checked with Archie to see what you liked eating, plus I added some staple items, the bathroom and laundry supplies are in the linen cupboard, and I've cleaned and dusted all the rooms."

That was no small task, my parents' house, a little like a maze. "Thanks so much!" I leant over and hugged my aunt. I didn't know what else to say. From my chair I listened to Shaun and Archie, and smiled at Kris, marvelling on how so much good could come after so much pain. It felt...nice...I didn't have another word to describe the feeling of contentment that ran through my body. If I closed my eyes, I could imagine my parents and my son in the spare seats, completing the picture.

"It's a shame you don't have a fence that surrounds the property. I'd like to padlock a gate, as an added precaution." Uncle Shaun's words interrupted my daydream.

"True," I mused, thinking about the logistics. This wasn't a square block, the garden rambled around the house. "It would take a lot of work, and I don't like the idea of people traipsing around the garden erecting the fence. Especially people I don't know."

"Leave it with me," Archie said mysteriously. He did know a lot of people, not just because of the café. My bestie knew how to network.

The memorial is tomorrow, I told Leo as I hopped into bed, hours later. Archie, Shaun, and Kris all offered to stay, but once again I declined. I had to get used to being alone in this house. *It's only a small service, here at home. Mum and Dad didn't follow any particular religion, and their funeral was technically in Denmark, when they were cremated. Auntie Kris and Uncle Shaun have done an amazing job. My parents' ashes have been turned into memorial diamonds. I'm not going to wear mine; I'll display it on the shelves in the main room. We've each prepared a few words to say. Eve suggested I could take the day off, but I want to go to work in the morning, and just come home at lunch, before the ceremony. There's only the four of us attending. The funeral announcement didn't specify a service. Kris and Shaun agreed that was how my parents would have wanted it. 'No fuss and just get on with living,' were their words.*

HOW I DESCRIBED THE ceremony to Leo, was spot on. Archie and I arrived at home in time for a simple chicken salad lunch. The four of us wore black pants, Kris and I chose red shirts, Archie and Shaun wore blue. Shaun, Kris and I each spoke, as we lit candles, on the makeshift altar on the sideboard table. Kris and I added a collage of photos of my parents, with each of us, and a couple of slender black taper candles in silver candle sticks, to the white table runner. Each diamond came with a pouch, a silver chain, and a display stand. We placed all three rocks on their stands as we reminisced about our lives with Tom and Dora. After many tears were shed, Kris put on the kettle, and Archie disappeared. "To check no one had damaged the café," he quipped as he waved, promising to be back soon.

Less than half an hour later, as Kris and Shaun reminded me that although they were leaving, they'd be back in a flash if I ever needed them, Archie returned. With Eve, and a huge feast of my parents favourite takeaway food.

AFTER MORE TEARS, HUGS and promises to be careful and keep in touch, I climbed into bed. Mr Ted snuggled beside me. Leo and my parents on my mind. A weird movie reel ran through my head. Me as a child, immersed in puzzles, word games, jigsaws, crosswords, any type of solo activity. I sat up, remembering the weird kid who'd sit in the corner and read while everyone else was playing handball. I'd be solving crossword puzzles while they played basketball and studying while they partied.

Even now, any social activity that involved more than two other people gave me the willies. I'd been called painfully shy, a snob, weird, and maybe I was a little of all of those. The doctor who delivered Leo called it post natal syndrome, and anxiety. Brandon used the words highly strung, and high maintenance, towards the end of our relationship, once he'd stopped the pretence that I was the best thing in his world.

EVE KEPT TO HER WORD to ask her friend Rosso to investigate the web of lies and deception created by Brandon. I'd provided him with copies of the misinformation from the safety deposit box and the deciphered shorthand notebook. It took him less than twenty-four hours to prove it was pure fiction.

Eve's friend had shaggy brown hair, and he wore an oversized t-shirt over baggy jeans. "I can't find any trace of Brandon, or Leo." Rosso saw the look of horror on my face. He glanced at Eve, and Archie who were also stunned by the statement. "What I mean is, we know they exist. There are birth certificates, and Brandon appears on the electoral roll as living in a rather flashy part of Forest Vale. He has the qualifications as a lawyer, and barrister, and is applying to become a judge." The four of us were sitting at my dining room table. We'd agreed to a Sunday morning get together, the only day we were all available.

I shuddered at the thought of Brandon as judge, dispensing punishments. The words *judge, jury and executioner* ran through my brain.

"Brandon has household staff, including a full-time nanny for Leo. He also has several questionable contacts in organised crime. Title searches confirmed houses in his name in London, Washington, Berlin, Tokyo, as well as several throughout Australia. Each house is huge and set up with full time staff. There are many other investment properties around the globe. Knowing all that, it's his precise location, that has proven difficult to pinpoint." Rosso stopped speaking and looked at me over the rim of his mug as he drank some tea. As much as I enjoyed listening to his British accent, his words were a lot to take in. I wished I'd thought to ask if we could record the conversation.

Eve and Archie also eye-balled me. Temporarily lost for words, I managed to state the obvious, "It's a lot of information to process."

Rosso put down his mug. "I've sources throughout the world, some virtual, others real. I look like a balding, pudgy, middle-aged hermit gamer, but don't be fooled, I used to work for an international organisation." His words triggered a memory of when I was little, maybe five years old. Of a group of adults around this table, talking in hushed whispers, while I played some game at the other end of the room.

"What's wrong?" Archie eyed me with a mix of concern and suspicion.

I gazed over at the shelf where my parents kept knick-knacks they'd collected from their around the world travels. "I'm not sure, I remember a group of people at this table, with my parents, talking quietly. I was little, I don't think I'd started school yet." My eyes zoomed in on a little white case, made of marble.

On my tiptoes, I reached up and gently lifted the box from its shelf. I returned to the table and laid the open box on the table. One item sat nestled inside on a red velvet cloth. A small wooden cube keyring, a small ornate brass key attached by a shiny brass metal ring.

"Have you ever seen that before?" Eve asked, as I gingerly picked up the item, placing it in the palm of my hand.

"Not that I remember, though how did I know to look in that box?" My hand shook a little, as I handed the treasure to Archie.

"When you were little, maybe you saw someone pick it up, or place it on the shelf, and your memory, or intuition kicked in when the memory was triggered." Eve shrugged. "It sounds like something out of one of our books."

"It does, doesn't it. How is this all linked?" I looked at Rosso, not expecting him to know the answer.

There was a task I wanted his help with. "Would you mind doing a deep dive on my parents? Anything and everything you can find on them. I think there's more to what's happening than we realise. I need the whole story." I felt Archie's eyes on me. I reached out and touched his hand. "Part of my problem is that I'm happy by myself, engrossed in the world of puzzles, mysteries within the pages of books. If I'm going to win the fight for Leo, I'll need to get out of my head and figure out the whole puzzle."

I held my hand up before Archie or Eve could comment. "Twice, I thought I wanted the anonymity of the city, and twice I've returned. It's time I figured this mystery out. I want Leo to live here, with me. If I must dredge up uncomfortable information to do so. I'm willing to. I am strong enough."

Archie looked like he wanted to hug me. I frowned at him, through watery eyes.

Eve passed the keyring to Rosso. "Do you have any idea what this key opens?"

The tech guy shook his head, "I thought it might be a computer key, but it's not small enough. What do you make of it?" Rosso turned to me.

"Not a clue. I'll pay more, if you've time to research everything about my parents, and their family."

Rosso stood. "No need for more money, or tea," he added as Eve collected our mugs for refilling. "This is the most interesting mystery I've encountered for a while. If I need any details, I'll message you. I have the basics, names, address, and I can find most other information from there. I'll be in touch." I let Rosso out the door, as Eve and Archie moved to the kitchen. I locked both door locks behind him. My fingers hovered over the keypad of the newly installed security system. It made me feel safer. I smiled. *Soon Leo, I hope to have you home with me.*

I HEARD EVE ON THE phone as I sat cross legged on the giant patchwork floor cushions reading a story about a hungry caterpillar to a group of six four-year-olds. I heard my name, and Rosso's. I concentrated on the story, and on the paper plate craft activity, trying my best to keep the butterflies at bay. Luckily, craft for the under-fives didn't take long. Their attention spans were shorter than mine. I left the children and their parents to browse our collection of books and toys.

Once the children and their parents were browsing the books, I realised my boss was absent. I ducked my head into the kitchenette, and her little office, keeping one eye on the counter and the front door. I couldn't get to the storeroom without leaving the front unattended. That door was closed. I doubted Eve had gone in there since the call. I returned to the counter and assisted parents who were borrowing books and toys for their little ones. Eve would turn up soon.

After the last family had completed their transactions, Eve returned, carrying two takeaway mugs and a plate of muffins. "Sorry for ducking out without telling you where I was. You were busy and I had to see Archie. Rosso has answers about your parents. Archie said you wouldn't mind if we all met up for dinner at yours, after work. I'll bring the dinner this time."

My spine tingled at her words. Less than twenty-four hours after I asked the question, Rosso had found some information. "Of course we can meet at mine. You don't have to bring dinner, but thank you, I won't say no, though it looks like you bought lunch as well."

"This is Archie's treat. Let's eat while it's quiet." She placed the goodies down on the table we'd made our makeshift lunch spot, when we were eating together. We could see the counter and were careful not to make a mess. I made a point of checking for and clearing any crumbs we left behind whenever we ate there.

"Did Rosso give any clues as to what he found?" I asked before taking a bite of an orange poppyseed muffin.

"Only that we won't believe it," she responded, taking a bite of one of the delicious cakes.

Chapter Twenty

Rosso was right. I told Leo later, after everyone had returned to their homes after an evening of dinner and revelations. Archie offered to keep me company, but I politely declined, assuring him I was okay, and promising to call into the café on the way to work.

I'd have never guessed my parents, your grandparents, both worked deep undercover for the government. Spies, but not in the traditional cloak and dagger sense. They used their real jobs as cover and travelled to where the government asked them to, to assess threats to our nation. It proved easy for Rosso to find this information, because Mike, no last name, who my parents reported to, was considering whether to read me in. What he thought about the four of us knowing about this, I wasn't sure. Anyway Leo, I have a meeting with Mike tomorrow. I declined to travel back into the city to meet at his office. He's coming here, to the house at midday. I love you my precious boy. We'll be together soon; I can feel it.

There was no way I'd be getting any sleep after that revelation. I held the mysterious keyring in my hand. I suspected Mike would be able to tell me about the key and answer all the questions spinning in my brain. My feet took me from room to room. Searching for hidden secrets.

The large cupboard at the end of the family room had been one of my favourite places for hide and seek during primary school. The room lay at the furthest end of the house, after all the bedrooms. It had been a parent's retreat, and a teenage one, as well as a place for family celebrations.

On the rare occasions I had friends over after school, we loved exploring the deep mysterious cupboards. Full of books, blankets, and odds and ends from my parents' childhood, there was always enough room for a child to hide.

I stood in front of the four-door cupboard that took an entire wall at the back of the room. Behind the wall sat the back garden. I remembered a conversation with my father, many years ago. I was a questioning ten-year-old.

"What's behind the cupboard?" I'd asked.

"The back garden," His reply.

"Are you sure? It doesn't feel like it. There's something hiding in between." My ten-year-old self couldn't explain it properly.

"Well, when you find what's in between, please tell me all about it," was my father's reply.

I'd spent the rest of the afternoon counting steps and knocking on the back wall of the cupboard. After the third round of measuring the outside wall of the house, and not knowing what measurement to compare it to, I'd returned to whatever mystery book had caught my attention.

Our house had been built in stages. I still couldn't work out where to measure to figure out if there was anything to my ten-year-old questioning. Rooms and walls jutted out into the now overgrown garden. Even during the daylight, I doubted I'd solve this by measuring the walls.

I flipped the light switch on the family room and opened the cupboards. The bottom shelves still held an assortment of items, though there was less than I remembered. The top shelves were empty. I shone the torch app from my phone along the back walls looking for a button, or a keyhole, anything to suggest there was something hidden beyond.

In frustration I closed the cupboards. *Just my overactive imagination* I muttered aloud. Frustrated I bumped the door with my fist. I heard a tiny click. *Great, did I break something?* I glanced at the doorknob on the left-hand side. Something was different, part of the handle hung to one side, revealing a small keyhole.

My hands shook as I retrieved the mysterious key ring from my pocket and slotted the key in the hole. I heard a small click as it unlocked, the four doors came away as one large door, revealing what looked like an office. As I shone my torch in the dark trying to make out details I heard a loud crash, followed by the shrill screech of the newly installed alarm system.

I closed the door, locked it, repositioned the door handle and headed towards the front of the house. When the others left, I'd made sure all the doors and windows were locked. I opened the door to every room and turned on all the lights. Nothing in the house appeared damaged, or out of place. My heart thumped in my chest. A panic attack, or a heart episode? Panic, I decided, as I concentrated on taking deep breaths, in an effort to calm down.

Turning on the outside light revealed the problem. Outside the kitchen door sat three tall metal bins, and some garden tools. Or at least they used to sit and lean against the wall just outside the door. Someone, or something had knocked them over, hence the noise. The security alarm still rang out, the shrill pitch hurting my ears. Standing at the pin pad by the front door, I tried to remember the four digit code. Uncle Shaun had told me, a number I'd remember. I tried the year of my birth. Thankfully the ringing stopped. The peace shattered a few seconds later as a loud banging sounded on the front door.

"It's Officer Dean, Are you okay Scarlett? The security firm called in the alarm to the station."

I cautiously opened the door, recognising the policeman's voice. Eve's friend stood on the top step. "Thank you, Officer Dean for arriving so promptly. Something bumped into the metal bins and disturbed garden tools that were leaning against the back wall. Whatever moved the items, must have been bigger than a regular sized house pet." My brain was still reeling from the reveal in the family room. Now someone was prowling around the house. I struggled to breathe.

"I'll check the perimeter, and inside as well, if that's okay with you. And please call me Eddie, Officer Dean sounds so formal. I always look around to see if my father is behind me," He chuckled, politely waiting on the step for me to invite him inside.

"Yes, please come in, and check through the house, and outside as well. I'll be in the kitchen, through here. Would you like a cup of tea, or coffee when you're done?" I led the policeman through the open living area into the kitchen.

"I'd love a cuppa, but I'm on duty, and I have another couple of call outs to follow up on," he replied, as he checked the window locks behind the lounge.

It was easy to see why Eve and Officer Eddie were friends. He was friendly and approachable, not rude and abrupt, as had been my previous experience with the police. His dark brown eyes had a sparkle and a genuineness that invited trust.

The coffee warmed and calmed me. The adrenaline racing through my body slowly abated. Gradually, the excitement at my discovery of the mysterious secret room returned.

Officer Eddie joined me in the kitchen. "Inside is locked and secure. The alarm will trigger if anyone tries to break in. I'll walk the outside perimeter on my way out. Is there anything else you need before I go?"

"Thank you, I can't think of anything. If someone was messing around outside, the awful alarm would've frightened them away." I sipped my coffee, allowing the familiar bitter taste to calm me.

I led Officer Eddie through the back door, down a couple of steps to where my parents stacked their most used garden implements. He nodded slowly. "I agree with you. This wasn't a cat or a dog. I could dust for prints, tomorrow, if you want to leave the tools as they are for now. You never know, we might get lucky and find some prints that are on our system."

"I'm happy to wait and tidy this tomorrow afternoon," I replied. There didn't appear to be any damage. Mum's rose garden was at least two metres away, down a cobbled path.

After Officer Eddie left, I made sure both doors were double locked. I left all the lights on in the main part of the house, while I returned to the cupboard at the end of the family room. I fished the tiny key out of my pocket, unlatched the trick handle and inserted the key in the lock.

The room wasn't huge. Four people would sit comfortably around the large wooden roll top desk that sat at one end. The other two walls were filled with shelves. I pulled the cord hanging from the light bulb in the ceiling. A surprisingly bright light shone across the secret cubby. That how I felt, like I was trespassing into a realm full of secrets.

On the desk sat a leather writing pad, a black leather container full of pens and pencils, and a blank notepad. The shelves that lined the walls contained books, and document boxes.

I ran my finger along their spines, reading the titles. Most books were named after people, or places. London, Washington, Berlin, Paris, Stokes, Williams, Edwards, Watson, and Kelly. There were plenty of others, I stopped reading when I saw Brandon's surname.

Hi Leo, it should've surprised me, that my parents had a secret room in the home I grew up in, but after the last few weeks, this wasn't a surprise. Neither was it strange that one of the books in the secret room appears to be about your father. I didn't read any of the information tonight. I couldn't bring myself to. I'm meeting a man called Mike tomorrow. He may have some more answers for me. So now I'm going to drink my calming sleepy tea, and read a mystery. Sleep well Leo. X

ARCHIE SCROLLED THROUGH the photos on my mobile. "This room was hidden behind that cupboard the whole time?" He whispered, his eyes wide as saucers. "Did you get any sleep, or did you stay in there all night and read?"

"I didn't read any of it, I thought I'd wait until after I talk to Mike. I got some sleep, after reading a mystery book for a while. I don't even remember any of my dreams." Archie knew about my nightmares. "I'm glad Shaun put up the security system."

Archie stopped scrolling the photographs and raised his eyebrow. "For any reason in particular, or just a general gratitude that the house is secure?"

I gulped down the lump in my throat, "I wasn't sure if I should tell you or not, and please don't worry, but something, probably a cat, knocked over some garden tools and set off the alarm. Eddie came up within five minutes. The security system alerts the local station. So that's good to know, isn't it?" I finished brightly.

Archie slid the takeaway mug over to me. "Hmm, I guess when you put it that way," he conceded. "Being cranky that you didn't tell me when it happened won't do me any good. Would you like macaroons, or chocolate fudge to go with that mocha?"

"A couple of both? To share with Eve?" I responded cheekily.

"If you promise to tell me as soon as your meeting with Mike ends, so I know you haven't been abducted or brainwashed…" he passed me a takeaway container already pre-packed with an assortment of goodies.

"One day you'll let me pay for all the times you feed me," I said as I collected the container and mugs.

"Not today," he grinned.

EVE EYED THE GOODIES I delivered to the kitchenette. "We'll have to start taking it in turns to go for a walk at lunchtimes, if we keep eating like this," she commented as she opened the lid to peek at the macaroons and fudge inside.

I groaned, "You're probably right." I sipped my drink, with an eye on the clock on the wall.

"Why don't you take the morning off?" Eve suggested. "I've got it covered here. There's only book club, and one high school class this afternoon."

"There's a couple of hours before I meet with Mike. If I leave now, I'll probably have to go for that walk, to stop me from going stir crazy. At least here I'm being productive. Anyway, I've an idea for a Book Week logo I wanted to show you." I dragged us both away from the sugar hit and unpacked my laptop on the front counter.

Two emails popped up. One titled *Stop trying to find me,* the other *No good will come of snooping.* I sent both to spam, blocking the senders, as I opened the document I was looking for. If my boss noticed, she didn't say anything, though I sensed a smile played across her face.

I handed Eve one of the printed copies of the draft flyer. "Did I mention I saw Officer Eddie last night? The security system my uncle installed sends an alert straight to the local police station. Someone, or an animal, knocked over some garden tools. My point being, we know the alarm works effectively."

Eve put the flyer on the desk. "I'm glad the alarm works. You can trust Eddie. He called in for a late supper last night and didn't mention the incident. He doesn't talk about work with me. And I don't tell him who borrows books." She grinned, before her face turned into a frown. "I'm not prying, but I saw the emails. I'm not worried for me, but do you think you should talk to Eddie about Brandon's bullying?"

My heart lifted as I realised Eve and I were becoming friends as well as colleagues. At least with my limited knowledge of friendships, this is what I imagined it felt like. "After I talk with Mike, I'll work out whether I need to go to the police. Oh, I forgot to tell you, I figured out what that tiny key unlocks. There's a secret room in our house. I found it last night. It was my parents' secret office."

Eve froze where she stood, as she was about to unlock the doors to let in the people lined up to enter the library. "Oh, my goodness, you did that on purpose, telling me now, so we can't talk about it, in front of our clients."

I couldn't help the grin, "Would I do that?" I closed the lid of my laptop and stationed myself behind the counter to answer any early morning enquiries. "I'll watch the counter for the first hour if you have admin to sort," I offered brightly.

Eve gave me a look that I knew meant she wanted a longer explanation later, before turning to greet customers with a smile.

An hour later, I'd helped a few people sign up for our library newsletter, locate the books they wanted to read, and in one case, show them where we stored the microfiche. Eve returned from the office. "Off you go, find out what you can. Take your time, I brought fruit for lunch, though that fudge is tempting."

The words, 'I won't be long', didn't seem appropriate as Mike hadn't provided a time frame for our meeting. I walked quickly, my family home was further away than my old rental, and up a hill. It'd be so much easier if I drove one of my parents' cars. I shuddered involuntarily, not sure if driving would be easier, or increase my anxiety. I huffed the last few metres. *You can do it Scarlett.*

It was unusual to see other walkers on my street. I didn't recognise the man, standing across the road, but he was looking in my direction. I hadn't noticed anyone following me, but I'd been thinking about the meeting with Mike. What details would he reveal about my parents? Distracted about the walk home, I'd not paid attention to my surroundings. Could the man be Mike? He seemed too young, more my age than my parents.'

Before I could over think it, I waved at the stranger and called out, "Are you lost, can I help you find someone?" The stranger put his head down, turned away and strode down the hill towards the town.

"Well done," said a deep voice behind me. I'd noticed the old motorbike in the driveway as I'd approached the house, so a stranger's voice in my ear didn't startle me. "I'm Mike, I'm sorry we had to meet, like this, or at all."

The man in front of me was tall. His piercing blue eyes met mine. I noted he was balding, with a peppering of grey amongst what was left of his dark hair. Dressed in jeans, boots and a long-sleeved shirt, Mike was exactly what I'd pictured as an undercover operative. "We've met before, but I was only four, or five years old."

He nodded. "Yes."

"Coffee, or tea?" I asked as I opened the front door and disarmed the alarm.

"Tea please. That's new, good idea."

"Uncle Shaun's organised it." I'd a feeling Mike probably knew Shaun, and Kris.

I boiled the kettle, got out two mugs, and two tea bags. "Milk? Sugar? I found the secret office."

"Milk, no sugar, and I know you found the office. We have our own alarm that triggers when it opens. Not when your parents opened it." Mike stepped back, opened the fridge and handed me the milk. "We also know you didn't touch anything in the office, and that there have been weird things happening around here." He took the mug I offered him and led me to the dining room table.

The room remained exactly as it had my whole childhood, and during my teen years. The dark wooden dining table, matching chairs and sideboard, the black and white lounge, the rug, and the side tables, nothing had changed. Yet everything was different. I was sitting at the table with Mike, a spy who worked with my parents for years.

"Tom and Dora loved puzzles, and mysteries, even more than you did as a child. They were recruited right out of university. I would have recruited you too, except they made me promise not to." He watched my face for a reaction as he sipped his tea. "Their assignments weren't generally dangerous. Corporate crime and espionage mostly. They uncovered an international organised crime ring and were close to shutting it down. The crime boss got spooked and disappeared. After what happened to you, they were determined to catch Brandon red handed. They knew he was one of the main players behind the espionage. They wanted to make sure he ended up in gaol for a long time. Some of us at the agency believe he was solely responsible for your parents' deaths."

I watched Mike over the rim of my mug, knowing he was watching me, for my reaction. "What's the agency doing about that?" I asked, as if we were talking about the football scores, or the weather.

"We're working on the intelligence gathered by your parents. I'm not authorised to provide you any details." He sipped his tea, his eyes not leaving my face, gauging my reaction. "While I'm here, I'll be taking all the files in your parents' study. You're welcome to use the room, however you wish to. I'll disable the alarms."

I nodded, not able to voice my thoughts.

"Is there anything else you would like to know?" His eyes held mine, searching, for any clue as to how I was faring with this unusual situation.

"If I think of any questions, I'll send you a message." I knew I'd have questions eventually.

Mike's mobile beeped. He read the text. "My team is outside. Will you give access for us to walk through the house, to empty the office? I have to formally ask you, it's protocol." His eyes were inscrutable. Instinct told me I could trust him.

"Formally, for the record, I give you and your team permission to enter the house and remove any files, folders, books and information that you need to." I fidgeted in my chair. Did I want another coffee? Not a great idea, but I needed something to do with my hands. "Another cup of tea?"

"Better not." Mike stretched as he stood. "It'd be an uncomfortable ride on the motorbike if I needed multiple bathroom breaks."

I opened the front door, before Mike's team had a chance to knock. A man and a woman, closer to my age than my parents shook my hand as Mike introduced us. "Silvie, and Brett. This is Scarlett, Tom and Dora's daughter." I handed Mike my copy of the key to the secret cupboard.

Washing up wasn't much of a distraction. I browsed the fridge and pantry. Kris certainly outdid herself. All the shelves were tidy. I couldn't see a speck of dust anywhere. The towels and sheets in the linen cupboard were folded perfectly. A little worn and faded, even the blankets were the same. I sniffed the fluffy purple throw rug. It smelt of my parents. The sting of tears welled in my eyes.

I returned the blanket to its shelf and shut the cupboard as Mike walked down the hall towards me. "We're finished here. If you think of any questions, email or ring me. Be assured that we are onto Brandon, and while it might take years, we will catch him." The key tingled as he handed it back to me. I clasped my fingers over the key and tucked it into the pocket of my pants.

"Thank you, Mike," I managed as I led him to the door. Mike bade goodbye to Silvie and Brett, who were already in their truck, and hopped on his motorbike. I sat at the table, watching them leave.

It's true Leo, your Dad killed your grandparents. I don't know what to say or do, or how to react. I want to find you and rescue you and take you away from all you've known, to protect you, and keep you safe, to love you and....

I felt sick to my stomach.

I saw Archie approach the front door and opened it before he knocked. He took one look at my expression and enveloped me in a huge hug. I swallowed back the tears that threatened to engulf me. I took his hand and led him to the secret room. "I found this part by accident." I flipped the handle, revealing the keyhole, and opened the door. "It looked more impressive with the folders and books. Mike packed them all up into a moving truck and took them back to the office, wherever that is."

Archie sensed I didn't want to talk about it. I loved that he understood me. "So, dinner tonight, with Eve? We can talk about whatever. If you want a lift to work, we need to go now, I've got Pippa to work in her lunch break, but the café will be busy."

"Sure, thanks, and thank you, for coming in and check on me." I linked arms with Archie, as I gathered my things, set the alarm and locked the door.

Chapter Twenty-One

Three more threatening emails waited for me when I finally logged on to my laptop. I sent each one to the spam folder, reporting them to my email provider. The titles *Stop, I see you,* and *I'm watching you,* didn't even raise my heart rate.

"Eve, do you think Rosso could trace anonymous email addresses to a specific location, or phone tower or whatnot?" I asked as the three of us convened for a late afternoon coffee at the Café. Archie closed right on time, shooing out the stragglers, so I could fill them in on my visit with Mike. I'd told them everything he'd said and reassured them that in Mike's view I was safe from any more of Brandon's bullying. The one thing I didn't share was the plan forming in the back of my mind.

"Probably, he's amazing with tech. Why don't you ask him?" Eve said between mouthfuls of melt in your mouth macaroons.

"Are you trying to chase Brandon's location through his bullying emails?" Archie asked, over the top of his caramel latte.

"No, yes, I mean I'm curious how people send anonymous emails in general." I hoped I made my question sound innocent. I shrugged. "Not a big deal, I just send his emails to spam now, I don't even read them. I am impressed by how quickly Rosso finds information. I might be able to find Leo by tracing those emails."

"Ah Scarlett the sleuth again, I see," he joked, referring to his nickname for me when we were at school.

"Mike's taken all the top-secret information. My plans are to settle into my home, fill out all the paperwork to start petitioning for Leo to live with me, and help make our Book Week celebrations the best ever." I sipped my iced coffee, relishing the sugary energy boost.

Eve glanced at the clock on the wall. "Apologies for bailing on our dinner. I'm meeting Eddie, it's his first night off in nearly two weeks," Eve's cheeks reddened as she mentioned her policeman friend.

"There'll be other dinners," I said with a smile. "We could even make it a double date. You and Eddie, Archie and I."

Archie raised his eyebrows. "Stop teasing," he grinned. "Can we still have dinner?" He looked across the table at me, sending tingles down my spine.

ARCHIE FOLLOWED ME to the kitchen as I piled the dishes in the sink. "I love that you are working on the project at the library, and that you are engaging through official channels to get Leo back. Can you promise me something?"

I turned to him. "I will try. What's on your mind?"

"Please be careful. We know what Brandon is capable of. I know you don't need me to stay here and look after you. Please look after yourself." Archie's eyes filled with tears.

Without overthinking it, I hugged him. "Thank you, Archie, for being an amazing friend. I can promise I won't do anything dangerous." My plan wasn't dangerous, but I wasn't ready to tell Archie.

Reassured that I wasn't going to do anything silly, Archie reluctantly left. I promised to meet him at the café in the morning. With a mug of coffee in my hand, I walked through to the family room and opened the cupboard doors. I'd need a printer, a bigger computer, a shredder, and other tech. I made a note to ask Rosso what else I'd need.

The layout of the room made sense to me. The shelves for books and files, drawers for stationery, and a long desk and two chairs made a great, snug office space. I could start my book collection and set up as a book reviewer. Reviewing books had proved a useful distraction over the last couple of years. With social media, and my library contacts, it had become an enjoyable hobby and one with business potential. A few authors had approached me, offering to pay me to provide a professional review of their books.

Returning to my laptop on the dining room table I ate some fruit while I gathered my thoughts. The doors were locked, the windows too. The alarm was set. No one would be disturbing me, and thanks to Rosso and the tech guy in the city, neither my mobile nor laptop were bugged. During his visit, Mike swept the house and confirmed the house was free of listening devices.

I punched in the mobile number on my phone. "You said you promised my parents you wouldn't try to recruit me. What about if I applied for the role? There's a gap, in your team, and it wouldn't take me long to get up to speed. My cover, er I mean my chosen career, apart from library assistant, is book reviewer. I'm working on the details. You know it's not about the money. It's not about my son, either, as much as about what happened to my parents."

"Are you finished?" I pictured Mike's expression from the droll tone of voice.

"Yes…" I couldn't think of a snarkier response.

"I can have the paperwork ready for you to sign by the end of the week. You realise you must agree to strict rules and sign a non-disclosure agreement."

"Yes, I figured there would be a lot of official documents."

"I'll send you some documents to read tomorrow, and Scarlett, I know you're aware of how serious this is, but still, I'm saying it, you aren't allowed to talk to anyone about your work with the agency." I heard the click as he ended the call.

I don't know what Eve and Archie will make of my decision, but it's the right one. I'm searching for you through the official channels, and also by continuing your grandparents' work. I don't know when I'll find you, but I will find you and bring you home. I'll never stop looking.

EVE LOOKED UP FROM the list of authors in front of her. "You propose to get all these people to visit West Haven during August, attend our event, and help with the activities?"

"That's the plan. I've already reached out with our draft calendar of events and all but two have responded."

My boss beamed at me. "I'm so pleased you're back Scarlett. You've such an energy, and great ideas. I love working with you."

Eve and I decided to surprise Archie by visiting the café after we closed the library. It was quiet, only a couple of customers finishing the last of their mugs of coffee. As they left, I gulped down the anxiety building in my chest. "Speaking of my ideas and energy, I hope you won't be mad, but I applied for a grant and won. The library will receive a significant amount of money to employ and train two interns over the next six months. I'm thinking Noah, or anyone you know who may like a career or further study in the field. I've drafted the proposal, and included the grant letter and confirmation." I slid the folder across the counter to Eve. Could she hear my pounding heart? It was deafening me, as I spoke through my pitch, before I gave in to my anxiety.

"You put a lot of thought and detail into this. I have one initial question. Why do you think we need additional staff?" Eve asked, as she read the documents. Archie quietly slid into the seat next to Eve, adding a plate of choc chip biscuits to the table.

"That's the other thing," I felt my stomach tighten. I lowered my voice, even though no one else was around. "If you agree, I want to follow in my parents' footsteps, on a part time basis. Apparently, my love of puzzles and mysteries makes me the perfect candidate for the role."

Eve glanced at Archie, "Did you know about this?"

He shook his head. "No," he said adamantly, "I'm just the caterer." He folded his arms. My heart sunk. I didn't want to hurt either of them, but this was something I had to do. Before I could think of a response, Archie continued. "I will say, when Scarlett puts her mind to something, there's no stopping her. She's always been great at solving puzzles."

"I am here, you know," I grinned, relieved by the brevity of his tone. "You're not cross."

"I am, and worried too, but what good will that do me?" He shrugged.

"You are more than just the caterer, way more," I added.

Eve held up the second page of the document. "It's clever, being a book reviewer, who visits authors. It's a strong proposal. If you're comfortable with social media, I think you'll do well."

My positive energy returned. Neither of my friends were yelling. "I thought we could showcase a couple of the authors, in the library, if we plan it properly. I appreciate you'll have to run all this past your boss, if you agree with my plans." I addressed Eve.

"It's a lot to unpack, but on face value, I support most of your ideas. Do you have a timeframe? When do you hope to have it all in place?" she asked.

"If we could announce it as part of Book Week, that'd be amazing," my voice grew stronger as my heart quieted.

"You're lucky she didn't say next week." There was a resignation in Archie's voice.

Eve gathered the folders I'd presented her and tucked them in her briefcase. "I'm off to get ready for an early dinner with Eddie." She touched my hand briefly as she left the table. I took it to indicate that all was okay between us.

As the door closed behind Eve, Archie moved to stand up. "There's cleaning I need to be doing."

I reached out, touched his hand, and held it. "I haven't always made sensible decisions, and I hate admitting being wrong, but I was wrong." My eyes held his gaze. My voice quivered. The energy between us palpable. Archie opened his mouth to speak, but no words came out. He closed his mouth. He squeezed my hand. "I'm not leaving you again Archie, I'll only be away for short trips. What I'm trying to say, badly, is, thank you, for being awesome."

Archie found his voice, "Is that all you are saying?"

My voice came out barely more than a whisper, "It's just, I think I'm ready to see if we can be more than just friends."

"I didn't see that coming," Archie said as he sat back in his chair.

Ignoring the blush rising in my cheeks, I sat down beside him. "So, I was thinking, after I set up my office, I'd sort the rest of the house. If you wanted to stay some nights, that would be okay."

Archie's cheeks turned the same shade of red as mine. He opened his mouth and shut it again. I couldn't help laughing. "You don't have to say anything now. I know I caught you by surprise. We can talk about it later."

Chapter Twenty-Two

It's exciting Leo. I can feel the change in the air. Good things are happening around me. I'm closer to you than I have been since your father took you away. There's good energy in this house. It has good bones. It's a place for a family, our family.

Sitting crossed legged on the bed of my youth, I thought about my childhood. Jigsaws, posh wine, crime writers, azaleas, and tennis – some of the memories I have of my mother. It felt like another lifetime. Wishing I had a mother who'd sit and talk about boys. She was always busy, never needing my help with the cooking or housework. As long as I worked hard at school, and obeyed the rules, both my parents were happy. I'd vowed to parent differently if I ever became a mother.

Having lost both my parents, there'd be no opportunities for mending relationships with them. I stared at the teddy bear propped up on the pillow. Did my child have a teddy on his bed? Was he being looked after? What would it take to rescue him and bring him home? Hot tears ran down my cheeks. I wiped them away determinedly. It may be too late to mend the bridge between myself and my mother, but I could still save my son. Regret tugged at my heart, as if someone stabbed me, and pulled a string tight. For too long I let anxiety and fear rule my life.

I've taken some steps Leo. I'm going to actively work on projects to bring me closer to you. For too long I've lived in fear.

I choose a romance book on my e-book reader. I snuggled into the covers and read until I dreamt of picnics and laughter instead of monsters and bullies.

EVE OPENED THE BACK door, smiling, as I arrived at the library. "Hello Scarlett. I've left you a note on the kitchen table. I've thought about your proposal and I've an early morning meeting with my supervisor to pitch your idea to him. All your ideas. I fully support your plan."

I dropped my handbag and wrapped my arms around my boss. "Thank you!" Although I hoped she'd agree, part of me was certain she'd think I was crazy. "If Mr Hill needs any additional information, I'm happy to drill further into the details. Oh, and Eve, the part about me working for the same people as my parents, that needs to stay strictly between you, Archie and me."

"Of course. All anyone needs to know is you're undertaking further studies which takes you out of town from time to time." Eve patted my arms as I released her. "I'll be back in an hour or so."

The library doors had been open for an hour when Mrs Mac and Mrs Paisley entered. Mrs Paisley carried a small box, Mrs Mac said something to her friend which I didn't catch. I smiled at my teachers, from where I was entering returns into our cataloguing system. Mrs Mac was tall, her short dark hair styled into a bob. My English teacher's grey hair and conversative clothing made her appear the senior of the two women. I didn't know they were friends, but it made sense, for retired schoolteachers of around the same age, to have similar interests. And lots of free time to read. Did they read the same types of books?

"Scarlett," both women spoke at the same time. They shared a glance. Mrs Mac nodded.

"We were devastated to hear about what happened to your parents," Mrs Paisley continued. Both women looked like they wanted to hug me. I wasn't sure if I was sad or relieved that the counter stood between us. "We are sorry for your loss, and if either of us can help in any way, please reach out."

"Amelia here," Mrs Mac gestured at her friend, "Suggested we cook some food and bring for you, but I reminded her that Archie often brings you dinner." I was surprised, I didn't know it was widely known that Archie looked after me.

"Suzanna reminded me how independent you were at school, and self-sufficient, when your parents used to travel," my English teacher's voice caught in her throat. "You're back at your parents' house now, aren't you? Did we hear correctly that the cute cottage you were renting burnt down?"

My anxiety rumbled around, making me feel nauseous. I swallowed the lump in my throat. "Thank you both, for being so kind, and thoughtful. Yes, my cottage burnt, and I lost most of my things. I'm back at my old family home, my home now, it's still difficult to believe..." my voice trailed off before I finished my sentence.

Mrs Paisley patted my hand. "If you need anything, we are here. Being independent doesn't mean you can't ask for help."

Mrs Mac handed me the small, gift-wrapped box. "Never think you are alone. There are people in town who are willing to provide help and support," she said cryptically.

I unwrapped the paper, to reveal a black box, a little bigger than a normal deck of cards. I lifted the lid to reveal a pack of tarot cards. "Did you send me the mysterious messages via tarot cards?" I asked my teachers.

"Suzannah did. We wanted to let you know you weren't crazy, and to trust in yourself. Unfortunately, when you returned to town, we didn't feel we could contradict your parents. They made it clear none of us were to tell you what we knew." Mrs Paisley glanced at Mrs Mac. "We'll always regret that. Gerald Watson is nothing like his sister. He lies and schemes, and his stepson Brandon is just the same. They bully and intimidate people and offer money and power to people who'll work for them."

"We don't know where they're keeping your son," Mrs Mac added, "But we've heard he's looked after by a lovely nanny who spoils him rotten."

I dropped the box of cards on the table and flew around the counter, enveloping both women in a hug. "Thank you," I whispered. "It's so good to know I'm not crazy." I believed my teachers. They couldn't be paid off by Brandon or Gerald. "I don't know what I need right now. You've given me friendship and honesty and that means more than a cooked dinner." I grinned through my tears. "Maybe I could ask for a posh dinner for two, to thank Archie for everything he's done for me, or cooking lessons."

Mrs Paisley looked at Mrs Mac. "We're more than happy to help, either with a meal, cooking lessons, and anything else you need."

As Eve returned to the counter, my teachers wandered towards the popular fiction section. "You have initial support for your projects," Eve clapped her hand excitedly as she relayed the details of her meeting with Graham Hill. "He asked for a detailed project plan, which I said would be no problem."

"No problem at all, I can put together all the details I have to date, ready for tomorrow morning, if that's early enough." My excitement bubbled at being given the green light.

Noah burst in through the front doors. Eve asked him to visit so we could chat about the possibility of an internship, if he were interested. "Do you know who owns the old van parked around the side of the library? Someone's rammed their car into the side of it and spilt red paint all over it." He flapped his arms excitedly as Eve and I followed him outside.

"I'm calling Eddie," Eve said firmly as I surveyed the damage.

"I don't suppose you saw who did this?" I asked Noah, not expecting he'd seen the incident. The one time I finally decide to drive

Mum's van to work and this happens. I felt surprisingly calm, considering someone had vandalised my vehicle.

"It was that crazy woman, Nellie," he yelled excitedly. "Her face was scary. She drove straight at the van in her little cube car and turned so her car dented the side. Her car screeched to a stop and she threw a bucket of red paint out of her door across the windscreen."

"Do you mean Nettie?" Eve asked, steering the excited Noah towards the library. He nodded, mumbling something I couldn't hear. "You can tell Officer Eddie exactly what you told us." Turning to me she added, "Take all the time you need. There's a hose in the alley. The council use it to water the flowerpots." The council had planted large flowerpots with rosemary and lavender and positioned at random intervals along the footpath. I took out my phone and took photos of the damage, the paint, and the tyre marks on the road. Hosing the car could wait until after the police saw the vehicle.

"You've had a bit of bad luck," Officer Eddie said as he exited his white police sedan.

I decided to hold nothing back. "It's not bad luck. A man called Brandon Kelly is deliberately targeting me. I won't go into the details now, but I'd like to make a formal complaint. Eve is with the eyewitness. Noah saw a woman called Nettie deliberately drive into the van, stop and tip paint on it. Nettie is working for Brandon, she's crazy."

Eddie stopped writing in his notepad and held up his pen. "An eyewitness? Did he say if she, Nettie touched the van?"

"She didn't get out of her car." Noah and Eve joined us.

"Okay, then if you want to wash that off before it dries, you can come to the station later and submit your statement." He turned to Noah. "Let's go inside and have a chat," he said gently.

I assessed the state of the van. I'd not be driving it anywhere for a while. Tugging the hose out of its wheel, I turned the tap and washed as much of the paint off the front of the vehicle as I could. I'd parked it facing the alley, thankfully, the watery red paint ran to the gutter and out of the way of traffic.

Eddie returned as I rolled the hose back into its case. "Call in after work, I'll be at the station until 6pm."

"Will do," I responded, my mind already ticking off what needed to be done. "Can I leave the van here, until I get it assessed for roadworthiness?"

Eddie handed me a card. "That's not a problem. If you call Wilson Bros and tell them what happened, they'll come and provide a free quote of what's needed to get the van back on the road."

Chapter Twenty-Three

Three hours later I sat at the front counter at the café with a mocha in front of me. Archie closed the door as his last customer of the day left the premises.

"By the time I got to the station, Eddie had already arrested Nettie. Apparently, she kicked and screeched for everyone to hear that Brandon would save her, and we should all watch out because he'd get us all. She didn't baulk at the threat of gaol time, maintaining the police couldn't do anything to her. Brandon didn't bail her out. He refused to take her call. Nettie broke down after an hour and named five others in town who worked for Brandon."

Archie hopped on the stool next to mine. He hugged me. "You're braver than you give yourself credit for Scarlett. Jai Wilson called in after assessing the van. It's drivable, no damage to the engine or the frame. He suggested if you take it into their workshop, they'll provide a detailed check of all the mechanics and fix any problems, free of charge." He handed me the key I'd left with Jai.

"Why would he do that?" I asked in wonder. I didn't know the Wilsons, except to say hello to in the street.

"There are a lot of people in town who are on your side," Archie commented, "Especially with everything that's happened. Your parents were liked and respected, and word of what Brandon is doing is spreading. People don't like bullies. I may have given Carrie some stories to exaggerate."

"That's funny. I'd never thought of telling something to a gossip, hoping for the story to spread. Very clever." I rubbed my eyes, my whole body felt worn, exhausted. "I don't suppose I could impose upon you for a lift and dinner. I don't feel like driving or cooking, but I'll pay for the takeaway of your choice."

"That's the best offer I've had all day," he grinned. "If you're willing to wait for me to clean up in here, it sounds like a date," he quipped. "You sit and drink your mocha."

"I can do that." I sipped the comforting sweet bitter mix.

"Carrie's a gossip, but she thinks of herself as my friend," Archie filled me in on his day as he fussed over the coffee machine, servicing all the fiddly parts. I didn't mind sitting in the café after hours. Watching him and listening to his voice was therapeutic. "She was in our year at school, then her parents left for a while and when they returned to town, she started her apprenticeship, as a hairdresser."

I pictured the blonde bombshell and gossip, her bust size wider than her hips, her big warm smile as she conspiratorially told tales to anyone who'd listen. "Which hairdressers does she work at?" I hadn't been into a salon since my return, opting to tame my unruly red hair myself.

"She has a salon studio at home, on Bailey Street. In her defence, she hears a lot of tales in her job, and I'd wager the stories are likely exaggerated in many cases. I normally don't pay her any attention." Archie scrubbed at a piece of metal, and little particles of old coffee grounds flaked off.

"But?" I prompted.

"She mentioned the altercation at the supermarket, between you and Nettie. Said Nettie had it coming to her, as she's been boasting around town how she's going to marry Brandon." He turned to side eye me, "But before you get upset at the thought of crazy Nettie being anywhere near Leo, one of Carrie's other clients knows Brandon and told her that he hardly spends any time with his son. There's a nanny, a good one, who's taken him under her wing. Highly paid and sought after, if Carrie can be believed. She provided the perfect opportunity for me to share with her what Brandon was doing to you. She was horrified. I got the feeling she'd be repeating what I told her," He added with a wry smile.

I watched Archie's hands, carefully wiping the grime and gunk from the tray under the grill. My fingers twisted the strap of my new handbag. "In this case I think I believe her." I told my friend about my interaction with our old teachers, leaving out the part about the special dinner for two.

"That's not the only bit of good news I have to share," Archie said, placing all the now clean items back where they belonged, along the bench at the back of the counter.

"Really?" I raised my eyebrows, trying not to fidget on the stool. I glanced at the clock on the wall. It was past 6pm, no wonder I was having trouble sitting still.

"Amy called in to the café. She's home for a few days and wanted to catch up with you. Her mother told her what happened, the parts she knew anyway, and she wondered if you'd be up for a visit." He touched my hand, briefly, returning to his cleaning seconds later. "She wanted to check it'd be okay to visit you at work. She feels she let you down, not returning to help you, after Leo."

"Wasn't she overseas at some archaeological dig back then?" I stopped fidgeting, and leant forward on my stool. Amy and I were close for a few years, it would be good to catch up again.

"Yes, she's been overseas for most of the past four years. She's only home for a couple of weeks. I think she'll call into the library tomorrow." Archie tucked the towel back on its hook, threw the dirty cloths into a bag, and collected his backpack and jacket. "Let's get out of here," he said with a smile.

I checked my emails while Archie plated our burgers and chips. Three emails from Mike sat in my inbox. The first email confirmed the names of the group of five people who lived in West Haven and worked for Brandon. The email contained enough evidence to convict the three men and two women. A quick telephone call to Mike authorized me to provide the details to Eddie. I sent the information onto Eddie via the email he provided me during our hour-long discussion earlier.

The second email contained the official paperwork confirming my role in the agency as trainee. "The role doesn't require weapons training or a fitness component, at least not initially. My role is strictly intelligence gathering." I told Archie.

"That's great, I couldn't see you succeeding in warrior training. Or brandishing a weapon," he joked, wiping his brow in mock relief.

"My first task is one I can do from here," I told my best friend as we picked at the big plate of chips in the middle of the table. Mike's third email comprised of a list of names, with instructions for me to put together dossiers on each person. "Like a test, to make sure I can do this," I told my friend.

I yawned as I placed two mugs of hot chocolate on the table. "Am I keeping you awake?" Archie grinned.

"Not at all. I think I'm going to drink my hot chocolate and curl up in bed with a book." I felt the blush on my cheeks as I added, "You can stay the night if you'd like."

Chapter Twenty-Four

When I woke it took me a few seconds to work out where I was. In my bed. With Archie asleep beside me. I slipped out from under the covers and tiptoed to the kitchen. I flipped the switch on the kettle, rinsed our cups and made us coffees. Strong coffees. We'd sat up talking until 2am at which point we fell asleep in each other's arms. I shivered, wishing I'd thought to put my dressing gown on over my pink pyjamas.

"This wasn't a dream then," Archie's voice had that husky, early morning sound. He slipped his arms around me. I tensed, then snuggled into his arms.

The whistle of the kettle broke our embrace. We laughed nervously. "Coffee?" My voice sounded odd; I felt the blush rise in my cheeks.

"I might just get dressed first," Archie said, kissing me on the forehead.

I watched him exit the kitchen. At least I had my pyjamas. Archie's singlet and boxer shorts were no match for the cooler late autumn mornings.

EVE AND I ARRIVED AT the library at the same time, again. "Great minds think alike," we both said at the same time and laughed.

"Book Week," Eve said as we deposited our lunchboxes in the kitchenette. "You mentioned having a school class involved in creating some posters and generating interest amongst the schools. Did you have a specific class in mind?"

I thought about the question. "Apart from thinking middle primary, the local school, I hadn't thought any further. Although now you mention it, I know one of the teachers, at least I used to go to school with him, Oliver Best."

"How do you feel about contacting him and having a word, then inviting the class in and talking to them about it?" Eve sounded tentative, probably hesitant to ask, after the van debacle.

"That sounds like a plan, I'll get straight onto that, and we can schedule the class visit for one day next week." I didn't blame Eve for the funny look she gave me, considering not so long ago I'd have run and hid from initiating communication. "Eddie probably won't tell you, because of professional confidentiality, but he's arrested five other locals who were working for Brandon. None of them considered for a moment that Brandon would abandon them, but I guarantee that's what he's done." I covered my mouth as a yawn escaped. "Since returning from my trip, I've found people willing to help. It's like a weight's been lifted. The work with Mike, I'm feeling positive about that too."

I considered cheating, and either asking Archie to contact Oliver, or wait and run into him at the café. Instead, I rang the school and asked to leave a message for Oliver to contact me at the library, during the day if he had a free moment.

Less than twenty minutes later the library phone rang. A group of senior citizens were gathered around Eve as she showed them how to search on the library computer. I took the call. "Scarlett, it's Oliver here, I was sorry to hear about your parents."

"Oliver, thanks for ringing back. The library is organising a series of Book Week activities, and we'd love it if your class would be our champions. I'll send you an email with our thoughts. If you and your class are interested, we can meet here one day next week." I scribbled little hearts on the blank piece of paper next to the telephone.

"I think we'd love that. Why don't we schedule Monday afternoon if that suits," Oliver sounded keen. I agreed and asked him about what authors his class liked. After I hung up, I drafted and sent the email invitation to Oliver and his class.

I noticed a text from Mike. Brandon vehemently denied having anything to do with the six people, including Nettie. Would Brandon take Leo and disappear? All I could do was keep working on my plan. There was no point in expecting the worst. A smile played on my lips as I remembered the previous evening.

"Scarlett!"

I looked up from the email I drafted. I recognised the voice and the young woman standing in front of the counter. I ran around the front and embraced her, "Amy! It's so good to see you."

After a few seconds she let go, "Let me look at you," she touched me lightly on the arms. "My goodness you look well. I don't know what I was expecting..." her voice trailed off as she realised what she'd said.

"I'm not doing too badly for a crazy, anxiety ridden, bullied, homeless orphan," I grinned mocking myself. "I stopped feeling sorry for myself a few days ago. Now I'm ready and willing to fight for what's mine. Enough about me, I want to hear all about your adventures." I glanced around noticing the library was filling up with patrons perusing the shelves. "Maybe not here, are you free for dinner? At Mum and Dad's, er I guess it's mine now."

"I'd love that," Amy grinned. I'll bring dessert." I felt lighter than I had since Leo's birth. Home. Friends.

"THERE'S SOMETHING DIFFERENT about Amy," I whispered to Archie as we snuggled under the blankets. "Not just because she's been around the world and discovered some amazing artefacts. There's a confidence that I don't remember."

"Arrogance, or assertive?" he asked, tangling his fingers in my red hair. "You could get Rosso to investigate her, or..."

I swung sideways so my face was centimetres away from his, "Or I could add her to the list Mike gave me and investigate her myself."

"I don't mean right now," he took my hand in his. "How about we set the alarm for early, I've got to clean the café, and you can get into your secret study and start sleuthing."

"Deal," I agreed, snuggling into the space, holding hands with my best friend.

THE WEEKEND ARRIVED taking me by surprise. I mean, I knew it was Saturday, and rather than being exhausted by the events of the week I was energised. Archie had bought over a toothbrush, and toiletries which sat with mine on the bathroom cabinet. Some of his clothes joined mine in the wardrobe and chest of drawers in my room. I couldn't face moving my parents' things out of the master bedroom, though I considered purchasing a larger bed for my room. The room itself was big enough. The smaller room adjacent to mine would be a perfect bedroom for Leo. Maybe I'd order furniture for his room when I ordered myself a larger bed.

Archie joined me in the kitchen as I plated up toast and cereal for us both. We sat at the dining room table, watching the sunrise out the window. "Kris did a great job with stocking the pantry and the fridge," I commented. "Let's pick a date and invite her and Shaun for a meal."

My best friend smiled at me. "Whatever Sunday you pick is fine with me." We'd all agreed on a Sunday as we could make it a nice long lunch, and no one would be needing to return to work until the next day.

"Call in to the café if you solve the mystery before lunch," Archie smiled, referring to the task Mike set for me. Our goodbye kiss sent shivers through my body. I didn't want to let him go. Finally, I released Archie. He kissed my cheek, before heading out the back door.

I checked the door was locked, and loaded a tray with grapes, berries, chocolates, another coffee, and a bottle of water. Butterflies jumped in my stomach as I unlocked the door to my secret office. Mike had arranged a whole room of tech for me, state-of-the-art computers not available to the layperson. With the tray of food to one side, a notepad and pen on the other I started my new role.

Four hours later my mobile beeped. The alarm I set for 11am so I didn't end up working through lunch. I checked my personal email and found a reply to my formal submission for custody of Leo. The department received my form and wanted to conduct an interview with me. The butterflies in my stomach started dancing. I didn't know whether to throw up or celebrate. I re-read the message and replied to accept their invitation. The department had a person at the local service centre and could fit me in this Tuesday.

Without hesitation I hopped into Dad's jeep and drove to the café. My mind was buzzing. It felt real. Having Leo back where he belonged. It was entirely possible.

"I'm surprised to see you, I thought for sure you'd work through lunch." Archie smiled. The café was buzzing with customers. Pippa handed out takeaway mugs to those waiting in line. Archie passed brown bags, containing an assortment of goodies to Pippa to accompany the mugs.

"I set an alarm, so I didn't miss lunch," I admittedly sheepishly.

"If you have time to take a seat, I'll bring you some lunch in a moment," Archie suggested as he handed tray of cupcakes to a young girl with plaits and a bright pink dress. He smiled at the father, as he helped his daughter carry the tray through the door without dropping any.

"I'm making us dinner," I said as Archie joined me ten minutes later. The crowd had abated, though the tables were still occupied. Customers with mugs, milkshakes, muffins, cakes, and toasted sandwiches.

"Okay, deal," he grinned. "How did you go?" He placed a plate of toasted sandwiches and two tall, iced coffees on the table.

I picked up a sandwich. "I completed the tasks Mike set me. I checked in with him and confirmed I completed them correctly. It wasn't exactly homework. The work I did helped with some active agency cases."

Archie munched on a sandwich. "And..." He always knew when there was something else on my mind, more I wanted to say. "Did you get the opportunity to look into our friend?" He said quietly.

I sipped the ice coffee; its sweet coldness sent a shiver along my spine. "I'm waiting for Mike to confirm. It appears that Amy knows Brandon. Her work is in part financed by him. The timing of her returning home, to support me feels odd. If she's working with Brandon..." I recognised the familiar anxiety, bubbling just below the surface. "If she is, I'll prove it, and even though I thought we were friends, I'll stop her," I finished. I drank more of the cold drink, pondering my words. I meant every single one.

"Wow!" Archie's eyes sparkled, full of admiration. My skin tingled as he touched my arm. "You are coping with this, far better than I thought."

I smiled through watery eyes. "There's more to tell. I've an appointment next week with children's safety services." My bubbly energy returned as I grinned at Archie. "I couldn't do any of this without you. Thank you, again for lunch. Dinner's my treat. After I get more work done." I eased myself out of my seat. The café door opened and a family of five entered. "Whenever you get home is fine." I wanted to kiss Archie but decided against it. I didn't know how I felt about public displays of affection.

Dad's jeep was easier to drive than I thought. With Mum's van in being repaired, my options were to drive or spend a lot of time walking. I grinded the gears, looking for second, as I got the jeep going. At the supermarket I grabbed a couple of items, planning on making tacos. Fairly easy, minimal preparation and cooking time. Setting myself up for success. I found myself humming rather than searching the faces of customers or averting my eyes. Had I finally reached a point where I didn't care what others thought of me?

I held my head high as I walked the aisles. Confidence was a new attribute to me. Other customers smiled at me, and I didn't care why they recognised me. Let them talk, and whisper, if my name was linked to Brandon's goons being arrested, all the better. I returned their smiles.

Back in my office, with another coffee, I set to work establishing my credentials as a book reviewer. Quite a few authors replied straight away. Another boost to my confidence. Was this too easy? I glanced around, expecting to see someone, who I wasn't sure, jumping out of the shadows at me.

No more ghosts, or running, no hiding, or letting bullies win. I'm not sure yet how I'll manage it, but I will bring you home. I'm not naïve enough to think it'll be easy, or quick, but I'm not giving up. Just because we caught five, no six people in town who were working for Brandon doesn't mean there won't be others.

I remembered the appointment next week. *With the support of children's services, I plan to bring you home.*

It was difficult to settle, my thoughts on Leo, my parents, and Archie. My instinct told me there'd be no threats would be coming my way for a while. Brandon was cunning, good at playing the long game. I could be too. Stubborn, impatient, nervous, but also patient, clever, strong...

Enough distractions, get back to work Scarlett.

Luckily, I checked my emails, or I would've missed Mike's email. I rang the number, as he instructed. "Your instincts are spot on," his gravelly voice echoing down the phone line. "I'm in a wind tunnel," he added, as if that explained the sound. "Amy's archaeological work is financed by Kelly and Associates, one of Brandon's companies. Do you think you're up for proving there's fraud or corruption? It would mean investigating your friend."

"Yes. I don't have a problem with that. It will mean getting closer to putting Brandon in gaol for a long time and bringing Leo home." A million ideas ran through my head.

"It's your decision, how to tackle this. You know the individuals and have the autonomy to make decisions. Put together a plan and run it past me, first thing Monday morning." Mike's voice cut in and out. It must be a long tunnel. The connection died before I could answer.

A glance at the clock told me I had a couple of hours before Archie would be home. A smile played on my lips, using the words home and Archie in the same breath. Powered by an energy I didn't know I possessed; I managed quite a lot of work in that time. As Archie opened the back door, he found me with the ingredients for dinner lined up in the kitchen bench.

"What do we have here? Scarlett Nightly cooking dinner from scratch? Not takeaway, or a jigsaw dinner," he chuckled, ducking as I went to swipe at his arm. I settled for planting a kiss on his forehead, no small feat as he was a little taller than me. "If I didn't know better, I'd suspect you were buttering me up for something," he pretended to frown.

Everything in the kitchen reminded me of home. I never wanted to leave it again, except if it meant bringing Leo home "I may have to leave town on a job, soon, but not for long." I finely chopped onions, hoping to mask the tears running down my cheeks. "Amy's work is financed by one of Brandon's companies. "The thing is, when I think of the home, I want to bring Leo home to, it's this home, this kitchen...with you in it."

The silence in the kitchen nearly made me lose my confidence.

Archie touched my shoulders and gently spun me to face him. "Do you mean that?" He asked quietly.

"I do," I my voice came out as a hoarse whisper. "You don't have to say anything now. Take all the time you need, to think about it."

"Yes. The answer is yes," he replied huskily.

The air around me was lighter than normal, my feet barely touched the ground as I busied myself creating the best meal ever. I refused Archie's offer of help, making him sit and relax. I took in my surroundings. If this much was real, I smiled at Archie as he read one of the books I'd left lying on the table, then anything was possible.

Leo, I'm bringing you home.

The End.

Sarah Lewin

If you want to know more about me or my books, here are some details. Alternatively, please make contact via any of the social media listed below:

Email: sarahlewinauthor@gmail.com

You Tube: https://youtube.com/@sarahlewinangelwisdom539

Blog: https://sarahlewin.com

Facebook: https://www.facebook.com/SarahLewinAuthorWitchyMysteryBooks

Instagram: https://www.instagram.com/sarahlewin_author/

Amazon: https://amazon.com/author/sarahlewin

Goodreads: https://www.goodreads.com/author/show/43342156.Sarah_Lewin

Book Bub: https://www.bookbub.com/authors/sarah-lewin

My Witchy Mystery Books:

<u>Witch Wisdom Series:</u>

#1 – *Crone Wisdom*

#2 – *Ancient Wisdom*

#3 – *The Wisdom of the Witches*

There are two free novellas in this series

The Coven

Kai's Story

<u>Spirit Town Cozy Mysteries:</u>

#1 – *Autumn Leaves Are Falling*

#2 – *Secrets Ghosts and Whispers*

#3 – *The Ghosts of Spirit Town*

One free novella

Beth's Return

<u>MISTY VALE COZY MYSTERIES:</u>
#1 – *A Very Crafty Christmas*
One free novella
<u>Stand Alone Books</u>
Broken Lies
<u>Anthologies</u>
Tales of the Lost Things
<u>I also have a range of children's books available, and some more cozy mysteries due for release in 2025.</u>